CURSE OF THE WOLF

PACK LOYALTY
BOOK FIVE

AMELIA SHAW

CHAPTER 1

MANNIX

My father was a crazy, A-list asshole. I didn't like admitting it to anyone or saying the words out loud, but there was no changing the facts.

What sort of man, let alone an Alpha shifter, would drive his eldest child one hundred miles from home, leave him in the wilderness, and tell him to find his own way back?

Because that's exactly what my father did to my older brother, Reid, when he was eight years old.

For years, the pack believed Reid had died. What eight-year-old could survive the harsh winters of our state? After all, my father had chosen one of the most bitterly cold days of the year to drop Reid off. At least that was what I'd been told by others as I'd gotten older.

Within our pack, people would often gossip and speculate on how my brother had likely died. He'd been too young to shift. Too young to hunt. So how had my father ever expected him to survive? The simple truth was he probably hadn't. Which made my father... what? A murderer? Insane? Or both?

The pack said my father was cursed. And when he died in a fire a later that same year, no one had been surprised. He'd killed himself and my mother. I'd only been five years old at the time, so I don't remember much about that time.

I was saved by my father's best friend and the man who raised me, Alfred. A kind man. A loving beta who took on the role of Alpha after my father's passing, only because there was no one else in the pack to do it.

But the biggest shock of all had come the night before Alfred died. He confided in me that he'd heard whispers that my brother Reid was still alive.

I hadn't wasted any time. In the same week that I buried the man who'd raised me, I set off in the same direction my father had apparently driven off in with my brother all those years ago. I'd traveled from pack to pack, asking everyone I met about a man named Reid.

Eventually, I found someone who knew of a man with an Alpha's size, height and strength. He was apparently quiet but a good leader. That description sounded just like the man I'd always envisioned my brother would have been. But was it him? And what would the passage of time have done to him?

I turned off the engine of my truck and stared out the front window at the buildings set around this village square. I'd been driving for a month, and I finally arrived at the Northwood pack grounds.

My heart pounded a little too hard in my chest and after all this time, I hesitated to get out of the vehicle.

Suddenly a fist pounded on my window, and I jumped, glaring at the guy staring at me.

"Can I help you?" he called out.

I sighed and pulled the keys out of the ignition before pushing open the door, my hesitation at an end.

"Hey, man." I shut the door and slid the keys into my jeans pocket.

"Hey," he repeated. "Are you looking for someone?"

My heart thudded again, sending stress bucketing through my system. "Yeah. I'm looking for Reid."

The guy's eyebrows fluttered high on his forehead and his eagle-like gaze scraped over me. "Oh, yeah? I was heading over there myself to have a chat with the Alpha. Wanna tag along?"

I inhaled sharply, a pain like being kicked in the gut hitting me square in the solar plexus. "Sure. I'm Mannix, by the way."

I held out my hand and the other guy took it, shaking my whole arm with the strength of his grip. "I'm Jason. Come on. They should be home now."

"They?" I asked, walking side by side with the guy who had to be one of the pack's betas. He was large and looked fit but was still an inch or two shorter than me.

"Yeah, the Alpha and her family."

"*Her* family?" I repeated. "Your Alpha is a… her?" How did that work? Didn't Jason say we were going to see Reid?

Jason frowned at me. "I thought you said you knew Reid."

"I do… kind of," I muttered as we stepped up in front of a large log house. It was double story and surrounded by gardens.

I glanced around. It was the only two-story house in the area. "This is the Alpha's house," I said, knowing I was correct without needing Jason to confirm it.

Jason frowned at me, suspicious now of a stranger, which made him a good beta. "I think you're going to have to explain to me what you're doing here before I let you in to see Allara and Reid."

"Allara?" I repeated. "Is that my brother's mate?"

"Brother?" Jason gasped, his shock visible in the way his frown disappeared, and his mouth dropped open.

I wanted to smack myself in the head. "Look. I…" I'd royally fucked this up. I hadn't wanted it to come out like that. "My brother went missing twenty years ago. His name was Reid. We all thought he'd died, but I was told only a week ago that he was still alive."

"So, you're here to find out if our Reid is your brother?" Jason asked. A grin stretched across his mouth.

"Yeah. Sort of." I glanced at the house, then back to Jason. "What's this Reid like?"

Jason assessed me, crossing his arms over his chest and staring me down. I must have passed some kind of test because he relaxed a notch. "You kinda look like him, you know."

"I do?"

Jason nodded. "Yeah. Same eyes, and that cleft in your chin. Anyway, Reid's a great guy. He's mated to our Alpha, Allara."

"Was he born in the pack?" I asked, hoping he wasn't and assuming that Jason wouldn't waste my time if he was.

Jason shook his head. "No. He was a foundling. One of our women discovered him in the forest, half dead, starving and dehydrated, when he was about ten."

Ten? Jesus. He'd survived two *years* out there, on his own?

"Or that's what we all thought because he was tall. They never found out where he came from, and he wouldn't talk about it. Was mute for months after they found him, but he came good."

Every word was like a punch to my heart. "They… you…" I swallowed hard, tears clogging my throat. "You found him?"

"Not me." Jason said, shaking his head. "Emma. She raised him."

I stared at the large house, too many emotions to mention running through my mind. "What's he like now?"

"Why don't you come meet him yourself?" Jason said, knocking me in the shoulder as he walked past me and headed up toward the entrance. "Come on."

I was rooted to the spot. How did I approach the man who

should be my Alpha? The man my father had thrown away as if he were trash.

"I..."

Jason groaned, turned away and knocked on the door.

Oh, fuck.

The door opened and a woman answered, a baby in her arms.

My stomach clenched tight in my abdomen, adrenaline coursing along my veins. I wanted to run. Away, preferably. And yet I couldn't move at all. Indecision froze me.

Jason spoke to the woman. I had to assume she was the afore-mentioned Allara, then they both started to walk toward me.

My feet shifted on the spot where I stood, and I was glad to learn that I could still move.

"Hi, there," the woman said as she moved closer. The babe in her arms only looked a few weeks old but was content and sleeping. "I'm Allara, the Alpha of the Northwood Pack. Jason says you're looking for Reid."

I nodded, swallowing hard. "I'm Mannix."

She smiled softly. "And you're looking for Reid?" she repeated.

"Did Jason tell you?"

Allara glanced at her beta. "He did. He said you might be part of Reid's family. He never talked about the time before my pack found him, so I don't really know what to say or do."

"My father was our pack's Alpha," I said swiftly, wanting to get the information out as quickly as possible. "Your husband is my older brother, if your Reid is the same Reid I'm looking for."

I sounded like a bumbling idiot, but I didn't really care. Well, I did, but my pride was a small price to pay if I got my brother back.

Allara smiled broadly this time. "I think it's safe to say that he is. How many other men are the size of an Alpha, but were found wandering the woods alone when they were a child?"

Jason frowned at me suddenly. "Was your father sick?"

"Sick?" I tilted my head, pretending to think about it. Mentally sick? Probably. But how could I explain that in this moment? I ignored the question for now. "My parents died in a fire."

"Oh my God." Allara's hand covered her mouth. "I'm so sorry."

"It's okay." I shrugged off her concern. "It was a long time ago."

An entire lifetime ago, for me. I barely remembered my parents, and from what I'd been told about my father, I was glad I didn't recall much.

"Okay, well, Reid should be back any minute. He went out for dinner a little while ago. He won't be long."

Allara's gaze slid past me, and her face lit up like it was Christmas morning. "There he is. Reid!"

She waved her free arm in the air like she was hailing a cab.

I turned slowly and stared as a huge man walked toward us. They'd said he was Alpha-sized, but this man was even bigger than I'd expected.

His eyes were dark as was his hair, and in his chin, I saw the family cleft that neither of us had escaped.

This man was my brother. I was certain of it.

He walked up and went straight to his mate's side, possessively sliding a hand around her waist while simultaneously dropping a kiss on top of her head.

Only then did he turn his attention to me. "Hey, I'm Reid." He introduced himself with an easy smile, not a glimmer of recognition on his face.

"Hey." I nodded at the large man, no doubt staring like a wide-eyed fool.

Allara frowned at me, then glanced up at Reid. "Sweetheart, this is Mannix."

I wasn't sure if it was my name or if he suddenly recognized something in my features, but Reid's face transformed. His eyebrows drew together, and his mouth dropped open.

"Man... Did you say, Mannix?"

He was staring at me now with suspicion etched into every line in his face.

I nodded. "Yeah. That's me."

"Jason, take Allara and the baby into the house for me," Reid said, and his tone brooked no argument.

He was all Alpha, from the commanding voice to the straightening of his spine, to the flaring of his nostrils.

He didn't even look at his mate or Jason, he simply directed Allara into Jason's arms and stepped in front of them.

Allara threw me a worried look before she did as Reid had asked and walked back into the house.

The aggression in his stance was sparking the Alpha also in my bloodline. I pushed down my wolf as he rose inside my chest. He wanted to protect me from the threat Reid posed. I'd been raised by Alfred to be the Alpha of my pack, and every part of me wanted to respond to the anger Reid was throwing my way.

But I would not fight him, no matter what happened. I forced my wolf to calm through sheer willpower.

Reid crossed his arms over his chest and stared me down as if sensing the struggle inside me. "What the fuck are you doing here, Mannix? What do you want?"

CHAPTER 2
MANNIX

My mouth dropped open, then my wolf flared back to life inside of me too quickly to stop him. And with that flare-up came the anger.

I stepped forward and only just stopped myself poking him in the chest. My teeth were bared as I growled at him. "What do you mean, *what the fuck am I doing here*? I've been searching for my brother. The one I thought I'd lost decades ago."

Reid crossed his arms over his chest. "Well, that kid died in the woods the way his father wanted him to."

I glared at him. "Really? Because I feel like I'm looking straight at him, so what does that make you? A ghost?"

Reid's mouth tweaked up a little as though he wanted to smile, but he tugged it down quickly.

"Mannix, I don't know what you're looking for, but you're not going to find it here."

"I told you," I said through clenched teeth. "I'm looking for my brother."

"Why now?" he pushed. "What do you want from me?"

I groaned and threw my hands in the air. Of all the different scenarios I'd run through in my head, this was not how any of them had gone.

"Because I only found out you were alive last week! And it's taken me that long to find you."

Reid narrowed his gaze at me. "Oh, really? What changed last week?"

"Alfred died," I said, the pain that sentence brought with it still fresh, still sharp.

"Alfred?" Reid repeated, finally dropping his arms down from the defensively crossed posture he had going on over his chest. "Dad's beta?"

I nodded. "Yeah. He raised me."

Reid's eyes widened. He was shocked. Good. It was about time he felt something of what was going on with me.

"Raised you? Why? What happened to—"

"Mom and Dad died almost twenty years ago," I interrupted. "The same year you disappeared." The year I'd lost my whole family.

Reid's shoulders slumped. "They're *both* dead?"

I nodded. "Yep. Dad set fire to the house and killed them both. Alfred saved me." I'd been unconscious for two days, but I didn't mention that.

Reid sighed and shook his head. "So, he really was insane."

"Pretty much." Just about summed it all up. So much loss and pain. And we were now left standing together, but with a chasm of what seemed to be impossible to fix space between us.

There was a long stretch of silence, and neither of us seemed to be able to break it. I opened my mouth to speak once, then closed it again.

What could I say after that?

As we stood there staring awkwardly at each other in continued silence, a woman came walking up to us, her sunny disposition obvious on her happy face. "Hey, Reid. Is Jason around? I can't find him."

She stepped close enough for me to smell her and I inhaled sharply. "You're human."

Since when did wolf packs invite humans to live with them?

The woman laughed, then stuck her hand out to me. "I'm Tammy, Jason's mate. And you are?"

I liked the woman's spunky attitude and couldn't stop myself from reaching out and shaking her hand. "I'm Mannix."

"Mannix? That's a cool name."

She glanced from Reid to me, then back again. "Are you Reid's family? Visiting town?"

I tilted my head at the human woman. "You can see the resemblance?"

She laughed out loud at that. "You're kidding, right?"

I glanced over at Reid, whose face had transformed into a storm cloud of frustration. Did I look like that? I certainly felt frustrated enough right now. "Yeah, you're right. There are a lot of similarities, I suppose."

"What's the link?" Tammy asked, ignoring Reid's scowl.

I waited for him to answer but when he didn't, I told the truth. "Reid's my older brother and rightful Alpha to my pack."

Tammy's mouth dropped open, and Reid let out a strange growl. "I'm not your Alpha, and that's not my pack. They've got you. I'm sure that's enough."

I glared at him, my hands tightening into fists. "I didn't say I'm not enough! I said that you're the fucking true Alpha of our pack, and if I'd known you were alive, I would have come and fetched you back years ago."

Reid and I glared at each other until Tammy coughed and cleared her throat. "Uh, I didn't mean to say anything to upset everyone. Sorry guys."

Reid tore his gaze away from mine and looked at Tammy instead. "Not your fault. Jason's inside if you want to go see him."

Tammy nodded and raced off.

I slumped. "This was a mistake. You're right."

"You can't seriously think I would just leave my pack—the pack that saved my life twenty years ago. My mate and child. I have a *life*, Mannix. You don't get to walk in and just up-end everything." His voice rose as he spoke, until he was all but yelling at me.

"That wasn't my intention!" I hollered right back at him, unable to believe he'd egged me on into a shouting match.

Why was my brother being such a selfish dickhead? In my mind, he'd always been the perfect one. Obviously, I'd been wrong.

Allara came running down the path, her infant child now missing from her arms. "Hey, enough yelling. I think you two need to come inside for a bit."

"No, I was just leaving," I told her, grabbing my truck keys out of my pocket.

Allara stepped forward and put a warm hand on my arm. "Please. Come inside."

Her words were soft but like with all Alphas, there was steel behind the softness.

I opened my mouth to refuse but she squeezed tighter on my arm. "Come and meet your nephew, Mannix."

My nephew? How could I possibly say no to that request? My heart squeezed so tightly in my chest that I couldn't speak. I just nodded and ignoring my brother, followed her up the path and into the large, double-story house.

Inside, Tammy was holding the baby and her smile lit up her whole face when she saw me step inside. "Oh, good. You came in."

I glanced toward the female Alpha. "Well, I didn't think it would be a smart move to say no to Allara."

Tammy laughed and Jason walked up next to her. "You got that right."

Tammy glanced up at her mate. "How about we give these guys some family time and we go pick up our little girl from your mom?"

Jason grinned down at his mate. "Sounds like a plan."

Allara took her now-sleeping son back from Tammy, and the couple said their goodbyes.

As soon as the front door shut behind them, Allara turned her gaze on me. "Would you like to hold him?"

I put up my hands, palms facing her. *Hell, no!* "Oh, uh… I've never held a baby before."

Never. Ever.

Allara just kept coming at me. "That's normal for men, but it's easy. Here, just hold his head and cradle his back. There you go."

I don't know how it happened, but between Allara pressing the warm bundle into my chest and her soothing words, I soon had my arms wrapped around my nephew. Reid's son.

I stared down at him in wonder. "I can't believe he's still asleep."

"Of course, he is," Allara said. "He's safe with you. He knows that."

I nodded because a lump lodged itself firmly in my throat. Allara didn't know me and yet somehow, I felt her acceptance. Too bad my brother didn't feel the same way.

"So, tell us," Allara began. "How did you come to be here in our town?"

The Alpha moved over to the couch opposite me and sat down. She indicated to the large chair behind me. "Sit."

I didn't know how I was supposed to do that while holding a baby, but I managed to hold him tight, then squat until finally I was seated.

"Phew."

Allara grinned and crossed her legs, sitting up straighter. "Talk."

I glanced around and realized Reid had also come inside. He was in the kitchen, busying himself with something. What, I wasn't sure. But his mate was in charge now, that was clear.

"I... like I told Reid... my parents died the year my brother disappeared."

"What do you mean disappeared? What happened to cause him to end up in our forest? And how far away is your pack?"

She was all business now, and I didn't mind. It soothed my frazzled nerves to answer questions rather than think of things to say. I had nothing to hide.

"Our pack lands are around two hundred miles north of here."

"Two hundred? What the hell was a kid Reid's age doing down here, alone, barely dressed for a winter's day?"

I glanced up from the angelic little face I'd been looking at and stared at Allara. "My father dropped him off in the forest and told him to find his own way back."

Allara shot to her feet, her eyes blazing as her wolf rose. "He. Fucking. *What*?"

"Allara, leave it," Reid called from the kitchen. He'd obviously been listening to our conversation, and he moved to the doorway to stare at us.

"You never told me that!" she hissed at her mate.

I looked over at Reid, who shrugged. "It's pretty hazy to me. I was half dead by the time Emma found me and you guys took me in."

Allara bristled and growled some more, then huffed and sat back down again. "So, your dad was an asshole. Got it. Go on."

"A crazy asshole," I corrected her. "The pack all assumed Reid had died, then that same year, my dad started a fire in our house, killed my mom and himself, and I was saved by my dad's beta, Alfred, who raised me."

She gulped, silent for a long moment. Then she said, "I'm so sorry. That must have been terrible."

"To lose my whole family in a single year? Yeah, it was. But at least I had Alfred."

I still remember the crash of the glass as Alfred broke through the window to drag me out of the smoke and flames into the cold night air. He'd saved me and the pack, that night.

"Okay. So, what brings you to this point?" she asked, getting back on track. "Coming here, to find Reid."

"Well, like everyone, I'd always been under the impression Reid had died. No one expected him to survive what my dad did to him, and I was only five at the time. When I was told Reid had died, I believed it."

Reid made a hmph noise from where he'd retreated to the kitchen, and I continued, "But last week, the night Alfred died, he told me he believed Reid was still alive. That he'd heard stories at town meetings and from other pack Alphas, that there was a female Alpha far down south who'd married a foundling. A man everyone said was an Alpha's size." I stopped to swallow the lump that had risen once more. "That he was kind and gentle. Quiet. But as loyal as the day is long."

The tears actually blinded me now, so I dropped my head and stared at my nephew. "The description sounded like how I remembered Reid."

"That is Reid," Allara said quietly.

I nodded, not looking up. "So, I made sure my betas had everything they needed to survive without me for a while, bought a cell phone even though I detest the things, and I headed south."

"To find him? To find Reid?"

I nodded again. "Yeah." The only family I had left.

CHAPTER 3
MANNIX

The silence around me was heavy and hot. Like a day with too much sun, a little rain, and clouds that blocked it all in.

Allara cleared her throat. "Well, you've found him, Mannix. You've found your older brother. So... what's the plan now?"

I sighed. I didn't really have a plan. "I don't know. The odds of finding Reid were so slim, I... didn't really think past that point." And if I had, I probably would have wanted my brother to come home with me.

Now that I looked at it properly, it was becoming clear that half-formed plan wasn't even a consideration.

"Well, there's a lot to discuss," Allara said, sitting straighter and taller, if that were possible.

"Like what?" I asked, then shifted position on the chair.

I must have done it wrong because the baby began to squirm, his little face scrunching up in an angry way.

Panic hit me and I extended my arms out to the female Alpha. "I think he wants you."

Allara got up from her chair and scooped up the baby with a practiced move. "Thanks. He'll be getting hungry."

She walked over to Reid in the kitchen and whispered to him so quietly that even my wolf hearing couldn't pick up her words.

"Back soon," she called out to me. "I'm going to go feed him in the bedroom." Then she disappeared from sight, and I was left alone with my brother.

I slumped against the back of the recliner, finally feeling the exhaustion from the week of travel. The high expectations, and the subsequent low outcome. What had I anticipated, really? For Reid to just welcome me into his new family with open arms?

I got to my feet, bone-weary. "Is there anywhere I can stay tonight? I'd head back to my pack now if I could, but I haven't gotten much sleep this week." And I honestly wasn't sure it was safe for me to drive at the moment.

The last thing my pack needed was another dead Alpha.

"There should be. There's a couple of people in town that have accommodations they rent out to pack visitors."

"I've got money, so I can pay," I confirmed, lifting my chin. "I don't need charity. Or, if you'd prefer, I can find a motel somewhere nearby."

"No." Reid shook his head as though fighting with himself. "Allara... uh, she wants you to stick around today so we can sort some shit out."

"What sort of shit?" Why did they keep thinking I'd come here with an ulterior motive?

Reid frowned at me. "I assume I have to sign something to say that I relinquish succession to the title. I don't want to be Alpha. It's all yours."

Oh, that. Yeah. Whatever.

I nodded. "There probably is, but I didn't bring it with me."

Hadn't even thought about it. Not really. I'd just gotten in my truck and left. Alfred had always said I was too impulsive, but I'd never agreed. Until now.

Reid crossed his arms over his massive chest. "You came all this way to find me and didn't bring anything with you that would let me sign over the role to you?"

I squeezed the bridge of my nose and inhaled sharply. I'd had a dull headache for a couple of days, but it was building into one hell of a migraine. "Look, brother, I don't really care what you believe or don't. I'll head home tomorrow, with or without your stupid signature. Just point me in the direction of a bed and somewhere I can rest for a few hours. I'd appreciate it."

It took everything in me to say the words with a little patience and not bite Reid's head off. He may not care one way or the other if he had a brother, but I did. Even a bull-headed one like Reid. His rejection was strange and painful, to say the least.

"Okay. Yeah. Let me walk you over to Amelie's place. She could use the extra cash if you're willing to chip in for food and stuff."

"Sure," I said, sighing heavily. "Let's go."

I turned toward the door as my brother walked past me. Then I followed Reid outside into the sunshine, blinking rapidly as pain exploded in my head. I must have groaned or something because Reid turned around. "What's wrong?"

I glanced down, unable to open my eyes fully now. "Migraine. I can't... see properly."

Shit. The flashing lights, the tunnel vision. I was in trouble now.

Reid's hand grabbed my elbow. "Amelie's place is only about a hundred feet up the road. Just walk, and I'll get you there."

I nodded and let him lead the way, though the panic in my gut was intense. I hated this. The vulnerability. I had no idea where I was going or who could see me stumbling along the road like an idiot.

It was the worst feeling for a wolf shifter, let alone an Alpha. Someone could attack me right now and I'd have no way of defending myself.

"Almost there," Reid said gruffly.

"Stop it. I'm fine," I growled back. He was feeling sorry for me, I could hear it in his tone. But I didn't want his damn pity.

"This happen often?" he asked.

I shrugged, tripping over something on the pavement, but Reid held me firmly and I didn't hit the deck. "Ah. Not really. Once or twice a year." Sometimes more if I was stressed.

"We're here. Two steps up to the porch, okay?"

I forced my eyes open to slits and lifted my legs to walk up the stairs. Fuck, the pounding had begun like a tiny pixie stood inside my brain, hitting it like my neurons were an anvil.

Reid knocked loudly and I leaned into him a bit. This sucked. Big time.

A woman spoke, and she had the sweetest voice I'd ever heard. "Reid. Who's this?"

I would have laughed at how suspicious she sounded, if it wasn't for the pain in my head.

"This is Mannix," Reid said, then paused.

I waited. Was he going to introduce me properly or brush over it like our connection was nothing? Probably the latter.

"He's my brother," he said, surprising me, though the anger behind the words hinted at the fact he wasn't happy about the connection.

Amelie's gasp was audible. "Oh my God. How... Why..."

"I'll explain later, but he needs your help. Can he stay here tonight?"

"Sure. I've got the guest room set up. But what's wrong with him?"

"He can speak for himself," I grunted. Then I groaned, destroying any illusion of being all right. "Migraine," I managed, and Amelie gasped again, loudly. I frowned in her direction though I didn't have a hope of seeing her. "Are you okay? I'm sorry, my head's so bad I can't open my eyes at the moment."

Which meant I couldn't gauge her reaction to a stranger turning up at her house.

"Bring him inside, Reid." Her no-nonsense attitude was one I was very familiar with. She sounded faintly like Allara. "I'll draw the blinds and bring you water. This way, Mannix."

I stumbled forward and Reid grabbed me again. Together, they managed to get me inside, with Amelie calling out instructions and Reid stopping me from falling on my face. Being inside and out of the sunshine helped with the pain a tiny bit, at least.

Then I was led to a dark room, where I sat down on a soft bed.

I sighed and relaxed my eyes so I wasn't keeping them squeezed shut any longer. The pain wasn't better, but it wasn't getting any worse, which was a good sign.

Amelie sat next to me and handed me a glass of water. "Drink this and take a couple of Advil." She placed the pills into my palm, and I squeezed them to avoid dropping them.

"They don't really help," I told her, inhaling her scent.

"Take them anyway. They'll help you sleep."

She smelled amazing. Even in my pain-drenched state, I couldn't help but notice her scent of honey and cinnamon.

"Have you been baking?" I asked to make conversation, then put my hand to my mouth and swallowed down the painkillers.

"No. Why do you ask? Are you hungry?"

I was, but I couldn't eat when I was like this. It wouldn't stay in my stomach long. "No. I didn't mean it like that. I can just smell honey and cinnamon. It's really strong."

There was silence around me. Why, I had no idea. Had I offended her in some way?

"It's a nice scent," I reassured her, then swayed where I sat. "I'm sorry, but I think I'm going to have to lie down." Before I did something stupid like fall down or vomit in front of her.

"I'll just wait in the kitchen." Reid said, and seemed to disappear, the room seeming bigger all of a sudden.

Amelie jumped up, then she softly pressed on my shoulder. "You can lie down now."

I did and groaned. The whole bed smelled like fresh honey cakes. Must be her detergent or something. "Thank you."

I lifted my legs and Amelie pulled off my shoes.

"I'm sorry they're not clean," I apologized. "And thank you for this. I... didn't time this too well, did I?"

I felt like a complete fool and must look weak to both of them. What sort of Alpha let himself get turned inside out by a simple headache?

"My dad used to get migraines. Bad ones," Amelie said, her sweet voice floating around me. "So I know how bad they can be. The water's on the nightstand next to you."

Footsteps sounded and I turned onto my side, nestling into the pillow, the scent now fading as Amelie walked away.

"Thank you again," I managed, the throbbing intensity in my head lessening as sleep called.

"If you need anything, call out and I'll come immediately," she said. "Get some sleep."

"Thanks."

The door shut and I sighed heavily. What a fucking horrible day. It had its perks, of course. My brother was alive, which meant my father hadn't killed him all those years ago. That was a great thing.

But Reid wanted me to leave. That definitely wasn't a highlight of the day.

I let sleep claim me. The faster I could get better, the faster I could return home and get back to my old life.

Such as it was.

CHAPTER 4
AMELIE

My heart was thundering a million miles an hour. The smell of Mannix, the sound of his voice, were too much for my starved system to take and now every single part of me was on high alert.

"Reid... he... ah..." I was shaking like a leaf as I stood in my kitchen, trying to get myself together. This was never meant to happen.

I put my hand up to my mouth, feeling the quiver right to my lips. "I..."

Too shocked to speak further, I didn't know what to say.

Reid, my Alpha's mate, stood in the kitchen nearby, staring at me like he had no idea what I was so worked up about. Even I didn't know what was going on. Not really. I'd heard of this happening, of course. But I'd never experienced it, not personally.

"Amelie," Reid said quietly, taking control of the conversation after words failed me. "Did you just... well... I don't even know how to phrase this question."

I wrapped my arms around my body and nodded my head. "He smells better than anything I've ever come into contact with. And the sound of his voice..."

A shiver coursed through my body at the memory of Mannix's voice. The moment I laid eyes on him I'd known something strange was going on, but after he spoke... Wow. Everything inside of me—my heart, my belly, lower down even—it all lit up like fully charged lights on a Christmas tree.

"Makes you happier than you ever thought possible?" Reid finished.

I nodded before I even thought about it. But how was this even possible? Mannix was a complete stranger. He had no right to make me feel anything at all, much less happy.

I lifted my gaze and stared at Reid. His eyes told me that he knew exactly what I was talking about.

"Is this how it feels?" I asked, a cold wave rushing over me followed by a hot ripple. It was like my system had kicked into overdrive and didn't know how to behave.

"When you find your mate?" Reid asked. "Yeah. Though I was only eight when I met Allara, so it didn't feel quite as intense for me back then."

I shook myself and stared hard at him. "Did you just say mate? I *had* a mate, Reid. You know that. And you also know he's dead."

Reid tilted his head and pressed his hands onto the countertop. "Yes, I know. You were mated to someone you loved, Amelie. But that's not the same thing as being fated. We both know that."

I trembled, adrenaline coursing through me. I needed to run. Shift.

"I have questions, Reid, but I need to go."

"Yes, go," he said. "I'll stay, in case Mannix wakes and needs anything."

The shift was coming, and without any control left whatsoever, I could barely speak. "If Lacey comes back. Tell her... I..."

I shook my head. Words were gone. He could see that, and he moved to the front door and opened it for me.

"I will. Go."

I allowed my black wolf to come forward, bursting up inside of me and taking over my humanity. I dropped to the ground, my skin sprouting with fur and my hands turning into paws with long nails that clicked on the floor.

My wolf took over and I didn't fight it, I just ran. Out the front door, down the road and into the woods.

I had to get away.

It couldn't be true. It couldn't.

I knew what Reid had been trying to tell me. That Mannix was my fated mate, the same way Allara was Reid's.

Fated mates had been considered a myth when I was young. Something only the rarest and most special couples had. But it was becoming more common, and often talked about in our pack and neighboring ones.

That was fine for them, of course. For people like Allara and Reid. But I'd never thought the same thing would come for me. I'd had my mate. My husband. My childhood sweetheart, Evan.

We'd been married for five years before he was killed in a pack war. My heart had been broken beyond repair, but our daughter Lacey had been only four years old at the time, and she'd needed me. My love for her was the only thing that wouldn't allow me to follow my husband into an early grave.

My daughter had needed me. She still did. She was nine now, and the love of my life. She was all I needed. I had told myself that for years, and I was certain it was still true despite the scent of Reid's brother that enticed me the way nothing had ever before.

I ran and ran, until my breathing was labored and my heart pounded even faster than it had when I first met Mannix and realized how special he was to me.

When I was finally exhausted, I turned and headed home again. I didn't know what I was going to do, but having another mate wasn't of any interest to me. And my daughter didn't need a stepfather.

By the time I got back to my house—the house my husband had built for me—I was calm. Well, calmish. Mannix didn't need to know we were fated mates, and he could go back to wherever he came from, none the wiser.

I trotted up the front steps, still in wolf form, to find Reid standing in the foyer waiting for me. "Hey, you okay?"

I didn't want to shift back and have to answer him, so I brushed past his leg on the way to my room. I did appreciate him waiting to see if I was all right.

As soon as I reached my room, I shifted back and shut the door. My skin was covered in sweat, so I jumped in the shower and washed. I could be hospitable enough, surely? I mean, Mannix was still likely out of it if his migraines were anything like the ones my father used to get.

I dressed quickly, in old jeans and a long-sleeved sweater. For some reason, I assumed that if I was more covered up, Mannix wouldn't be able to sense the truth. As I left the room, I checked my hair, and pulled it up into a high ponytail.

When I was finally satisfied that I looked presentable but in no way sexy, I walked out of my bedroom and into the family room once more. The Alpha's mate was still standing in my kitchen.

"Thank you so much for staying, Reid. Has Lacey come home yet?"

He shook his head. "No. It's just been me, here alone. Other than Mannix, of course, but I checked a little while ago. He's still sleeping."

I grinned at him. "Alone? You make that sound like a horrendous thing."

Personally, I kind of liked being alone.

He crossed his arms over his chest. "I've never liked being alone. Not since I was a kid."

I nodded and sighed. "Yeah, I get that."

Reid had been abandoned by his family and found by our pack. He'd been alone for a long time, wandering around trying to survive the elements and hunger. Probably trying to make his way back to his pack, the poor kid.

"Are you sure it's okay for Mannix to stay here?" Reid asked. "If you're not comfortable..."

"No. I'll be okay. It won't be for long." Surely, he'd want to go home soon?

Reid nodded his head. "Once he's better, I'll sign whatever I need to, and he can go back to his own pack and be the rightful Alpha."

I swallowed hard, my throat thickening with emotion. "He's the Alpha of his pack?"

Reid grunted. "Yeah, he is."

There was definitely a story there, but not one Reid wanted to talk about, obviously. "Okay, well, I'll let him sleep and look after him until he's better. You go home to your mate and new baby."

Reid walked to my front door. "All right. But come get me if you need me."

"I will." I showed him out the door.

Once Reid left, taking his bristling energy with him, I could breathe a little easier. Not long after, there was a little knock on the door. "Mommy."

"Oh!" I twisted around and opened the door for my little girl. "Hey, baby."

She rolled her eyes at me. "Not a baby."

I laughed. "I know. But you're *my* baby, and you'll always be my baby. Now tell me, how was school?"

Lacey chattered away while I made her an after-school snack, and I was grateful for the way she filled the silence. It went at least a little way to curb the storm of emotions and uncertainty that currently raged through me.

"Mom?" Lacey asked suddenly.

"Yeah, bub?"

"Is there someone here?"

I turned from where I was chopping vegetables for dinner. My stomach twisted and I reminded myself that I hadn't done anything wrong.

"Yeah, sweetie. Reid's younger brother is staying with our pack for a few days, and they told him he could rent a room here."

Lacey tilted her head, obviously confused. "Reid's brother? I didn't know Reid had a family."

"Yeah, Reid didn't either, apparently," came a deep voice from the hallway.

Lacey and I both twisted to see Mannix standing in the kitchen entrance, squinting so hard I could barely see his features.

I swallowed the sudden lump in my throat and put a smile on my face for my daughter's sake. "Lacey, this is Mannix. Mannix, I'm not sure if you can see her, but this is my nine year old daughter, Lacey."

I gave him her age details so he could curb his language if necessary.

He smiled and inclined his head. "Nice to meet you, Lacey. I'm sorry I look like this, but I still can't quite open my eyes."

Lacey hopped straight off her seat and went to him, reaching for his hand so quickly it made Mannix and me both jump. "It's okay. Do you need my help?" she asked.

Hot tears burned in my eyes. Lacey had never shown any affection toward a man other than her father. I couldn't believe she'd run straight up to him like that.

"I'm fine, Lacey. I just need your mom to show me where the bathroom is. Then I'll climb back into bed."

I walked over to him, anxious to separate my daughter from him. "I'll show you."

"I can show him, Mom." Lacey turned Mannix around. "What's wrong with you?"

I reached for her. "Oh, honey, that's not appropriate to ask."

"I've got a migraine, Lacey," Mannix told her gently, not moving his feet despite Lacey's insistence. "But I'd prefer if your mom took me. Is that okay?"

Her face scrunched up. "If she has to."

My heart lurched at her obvious disappointment. "How about you make Mannix a sandwich, and we'll meet you in the guest room?"

"Oh, yeah!" Lacey said, jumping up and down. "Do you like peanut butter and jelly?"

"Love it," Mannix said, with more of a grimace than a smile.

"Okay!" She raced off.

I took Mannix's hand, shivering at the instant electric attraction that pulsed through my body at the slightest touch. "Thank you for being so kind to her."

He shrugged. "Seems like a nice kid. Sorry I'm such a nuisance."

I led him down the hall. "The bathroom's here, to your left. Walk forward. And toilet's just in front of you."

For one single moment I considered asking him if he needed help with his pants, then backed up toward the door so fast I whacked my shoulder on the door frame, my face aflame. "I'll wait for you outside. Then help you back to bed, okay?"

He nodded, fumbling with his jeans. "Thanks so much, Amelie."

I turned away and wrapped my arms around myself, a strange sort of squeal lodged in my chest.

When I was around Mannix I felt more alive than I had in more years that I could count. And although it was fucking terrifying, I had to admit it was also exciting.

CHAPTER 5

MANNIX

After forcing down the sandwich made by Lacey, I fell asleep. When I woke up, I could tell several hours had passed. The pain had lifted but there was that horrible hung-over effect still weighing me down. I rolled out of bed, needing to piss again and stinking of sweat.

Definitely need a shower.

I stumbled to the bedroom door and opened it. The house was blessedly dark, except for a small light on down the hall. I followed the light and found the woman I assumed was Amelie, reading under a lamp, curled up on the sofa.

"Hey," I croaked out.

She jumped, her face flashing with surprise before she said, "You scared me."

I smiled. "Sorry. I was just wondering if I could take a shower, please?"

Now that the migraine was beginning to clear, I could see she was a lot prettier than I'd realized, with long dark hair, bright eyes, and a heart-shaped face. When she got to her feet smoothly, gracefully, I was hit with a deep longing I'd never felt before. I rubbed my chest where my heart ached and coughed to try and clear the strange sensation.

"I'll get you some clean towels and show you where everything is."

I nodded, unable to respond while my wolf growled, unsettled within me.

She walked me to the same bathroom I'd used before and began pointing out the soap and towels.

"Thank you, Amelie. I really can't... tell you... how much I appreciate this." I could barely talk and sounded like an idiot, but she just smiled at me.

"I'll get you some water and a proper dinner. Take your time." She left the bathroom and closed the door.

I groaned and sank onto the toilet seat, not sure what to do with all the emotions pulsing through me.

Was I that starved for female companionship that I was hitting on the woman who was being paid to look after me? Surely not.

I forced myself to my feet and turned on the shower. Time to wash away several days of stress and grief. I might smell a bit better for my host as well.

After my shower, where I spent half the time aroused surrounded by Amelie's scent, I climbed out and dried off. What was wrong with me? A migraine had never caused heart flutters and a hard-on before.

"Shit." My fresh clothes were in my car, a long way from here.

I wrapped the towel around my waist and ventured out into the quiet house. Amelie was in the kitchen, doing dishes. The smell of comfort food was in the air.

"Hi, I, uh…" I ran my hand through my wet hair and gave her a bashful smile. I had to work really hard not to let my body spring to attention the moment she laid eyes on me. "I didn't bring any clothes with me. I'm sorry. My bag's in my truck. At your Alpha's house."

Amelie stared at me like she'd never seen a man before. Her eyes were wide, and her mouth hung partly open.

"Are you okay?" I asked her.

She was a wolf shifter, just like me. We were used to seeing people naked; it was part of the culture of our people. I might have an Alpha's physique, but beyond that, I was sure there was nothing special about me to cause that expression on her face.

She nodded suddenly and began moving around the room, almost frenetic as she tidied things that didn't need tidying. "I've made a meatloaf with mashed potatoes, gravy and corn for your dinner. Come eat, and I'll run down to Allara's place for your clothes."

I took a step toward the bedroom. "I can get them."

"No!" she practically yelled at me. "Don't go out like that, I'll… I have to chat with Allara about pack business anyway. It's fine. Just get me your car keys and I'll go."

She was acting nervous and weird. I wasn't sure why, but I did what she asked. I grabbed my truck keys from my room and slid them onto the kitchen counter for her.

"Sorry I couldn't put my old clothes back on. They were past it a few days ago."

Amelie took the keys and pushed a plate with a large piece serve of meatloaf over to me. "You eat. I won't be long."

She dashed away quickly and I sat on the kitchen stool, the scent of a well-seasoned meatloaf drifting up to entice my senses. I groaned as my stomach twisted and turned. I hadn't had a home-cooked meal for a few weeks, and this smelled incredible.

I dug in, polishing off my plate before she came back. It was perfect. Creamy mashed potatoes, buttery corn. "Yum."

I carried the plate to the sink, washed the dishes, then poured myself a glass of water. The cold liquid was refreshing and perfect against my hot throat and dehydrated body.

When the front door opened again, I made sure the towel was secured properly and turned to face her.

She was holding my duffle bag, her face pink from running, I assumed.

"Thanks so much." I held my towel knot in one hand and reached for the bag with my other. "I'll go get dressed. What time is it?"

"About ten o'clock," she answered, swallowing hard. "I'll be up for a little while if you wanna talk. Otherwise, I've got some more ibuprofen if you want to go straight back to bed."

Only if you'll join me.

The errant thought came out of nowhere and I turned away, annoyed at myself once more for lusting after a woman who was obviously just trying to be a good hostess. And she was likely involved with someone already. After all, she had a child.

"Will your husband be home soon? I don't want to upset anyone with my presence."

When she didn't immediately respond, I flicked my gaze back to her face to find she'd paled.

"Um... my husband died five years ago. So, you won't upset anyone if you want to just sit and talk. I can make hot cocoa?"

I sighed, a sense of relaxation unexpectedly washing over me. It had been a while since someone had made me a hot drink and wanted to sit and chat. It was one of the things I would miss about Alfred when I got back home—our quiet camaraderie in the evenings.

"That would be great actually, thanks. I'll be right back."

I went to my room, changed into sweatpants and a t-shirt, and returned to the living room to find her placing hot drinks on the coffee table.

"Here you go." She gestured to one of the mugs, then immediately slid into the recliner chair, leaving the sofa for me.

I sat, feeling the ache of my migraine still present in my head. "Thanks for this. You have no idea how nice it is just to stop for a minute."

She tucked her legs up under her like a teenager and smiled at me. "You've had a rough couple of weeks?"

I laughed but the sound was brittle. "Ah, yeah. My parents died when I was little, and the man who raised me—Alfred—died just over a week ago." I paused to consider the date. "Actually, around two weeks ago now. I've been on the go pretty much ever since. He told me about Reid being alive the night before he passed."

I reached for the mug of cocoa and took a sip. Perfect. Not too sweet, but the milk was creamy.

"I'm so sorry," Amelie said, taking her hair out of the ponytail it was pulled up in and tucking her long, dark brown hair behind her ears.

She looked younger with her hair down, and even prettier. Damn it.

"It's okay. He was a great surrogate father. But he was old and in pain at the end. On his deathbed, when he told me he thought Reid was still alive, I was so angry at him." I shook my head. "I shouldn't have been. I know he was only trying to protect me, but it was wrong to keep that from me. I could have found my brother years earlier, if I'd had any idea."

She smiled softly. "You were lied to your whole life. That's bound to hurt. Anger is understandable in those circumstances. Must have been tough."

"It was. But I gave Alfred a respectful send-off, made sure my pack would be okay without me there for a while, and headed off to find my big brother." I grimaced. The outcome of my journey had not exactly been what I planned.

"Well, you found him," she said in a matter-of-fact tone.

I nodded. "Yep, I did."

"Then why are you so upset?"

I stared at her. Didn't she know? "Because my brother wants nothing to do with me. He thinks I'm here to fight him for Alpha or something."

I tsked, disgusted with the very idea of it.

"You're Alpha-born?" Her tone was strange. High.

"Yeah." I shrugged. "Reid's the Alpha. I was just the spare." I'd never felt like the Alpha of my pack. Did I love my people? Would I die for my pack? Absolutely. But did I feel right in my position? No.

"You don't sound like you want the job."

I stared at her. Was that a question? "I don't have a choice. It's my responsibility to look after my pack, especially now that Alfred's gone."

"It's a lot to deal with," she said. "Losing your adoptive father, then dealing with Reid's…" She trailed off as though she didn't know how to finish that sentence.

"Rejection?" I finished it for her, my tone bitter.

She shook her head. "I don't think it's a rejection. He just… doesn't know how to process it all."

I huffed out a laugh, though none of this was funny. "Yeah. Whatever."

"I didn't mean it in an offensive way." She sighed. "I was here when they found Reid. I'm a few years older than him, and I—"

"You're kidding," I interrupted, shock running through me. "You look about twenty-five!" My age.

She grinned. "Thanks, but I'm thirty-two."

I nodded slowly. The older woman, huh?

"Anyway, I was here when they found him," she said. "Half frozen, pale as death. He didn't speak for months. It was like he'd died out there, the soul of him anyway. But his body had kept walking, determined to save him." She shook her head. "It was horrible."

"It *was* horrible," I repeated. "What my father did to him was inexcusable."

"Your father?" She blinked at me like an owl, her eyes wide and shocked.

I nodded. "Yep. He left Reid in the middle of nowhere, then came home and killed my mother and himself in a fire later that same year."

We were cursed, my family. Reid had managed to rebuild his life, and I'd only survived because Alfred had saved me. And now that he was gone, I wasn't sure what I was going to do.

"But you survived," she whispered.

"I wasn't meant to," I told her. "I should have died in that fire too. Alfred pulled me out and saved me."

There was a long silence. What was she thinking? That I should never have come looking for my brother? Yeah, that was what I was thinking now, too.

When I couldn't handle the silence any longer, I got to my feet. "Thank you so much for the care you've shown me today, Amelie, but I think I'll go to bed. I've got a long drive back home tomorrow."

She hopped up too. "You're leaving that soon? I was under the impression from Reid you'd be here a couple of days. He said something about paperwork needing signatures?"

I shrugged. "No one wants me here, least of all my brother. So, I think it's best for all of us if I return to my own pack."

"Do you have a wife?" she asked suddenly. "A mate?"

I shook my head. "No. I don't." I'd never been interested in tying a woman down to my cursed family. And if I ever had a child, would the madness of my father flow on down to them through my genes?

It wasn't worth the risk.

"Good night," I said to her, my head swimming in the strange way that I'd begun to identify with being near Amelie.

"I'll come with you and change your sheets." She hurried to stand next to me. "Nothing worse than climbing into a set of dirty sheets after a clean shower."

I smiled at her kindness. "Yeah, but I was the one who made the sheets dirty." I was certain that those sheets had been clean before I ruined them.

She kept walking past me. "Just give me a minute."

She grabbed fresh linen out of a closet in the hallway and headed into my bedroom.

I pressed a hand to my head, the pain from the post-migraine stage coming back in force now that Amelie had moved away.

I couldn't figure out if she had some sort of magical healing gift, or if there was something more significant going on here. My head was too fuzzy still.

When I swayed with exhaustion, I decided it was time to follow her.

She was just fluffing up the blankets when I walked into the room, her scent filling the air and making my wolf dance inside my chest.

"Thank you. Again." I rested against the door frame. "You've been really great about this."

She gathered up all the dirty linens, holding them in her arms. "No problem. I've been happy to help."

She went to move past me and my wolf leapt within me, forcing a growl from my throat.

Amelie jumped back into my room, and I shook myself. "I'm so sorry. I don't even know what caused that."

Her mouth quivered as she forced a smile. "It's okay. You've had a difficult few days."

"Yeah, that must be it."

This time she slipped past me without incident, and I forced myself to climb between into the freshly made bed and rest. My heart pounded, and my wolf clamored to be heard. There was something special about that woman, but I had no idea what it was.

CHAPTER 6
AMELIE

I practically ran to the laundry room after almost getting trapped in Mannix's bedroom by his wolf.

The last thing I needed was for my wolf to bond with his. Then I'd be fucked, both literally and figuratively. There'd be no escaping fate then.

Instead, I ran from him as fast as I could. I washed the sheets, went to bed, and spent a fitful night trying to get some sleep.

By the time the sun rose, I was exhausted, but I could hear Lacey getting up and moving around. I didn't want her running into a half-naked Mannix, so I hauled myself out of bed to make her breakfast.

"Good morning, baby," I greeted her as I entered the kitchen. She was already dressed for school, which was great. "What would you like for breakfast? Waffles? Toast? Bacon and eggs?"

"Is Mannix coming out for breakfast?" she asked, her face alight in a way I'd never seen before.

"Why, sweetie?"

"I just wanted to see him before I went to school, that's all."

I tilted my head at her, not sure how to approach that. "Well, Mannix could sleep a lot today, honey. He was in a lot of pain yesterday. How about you come eat, and if he gets up, then great. If he doesn't, you might see him later."

Assuming he didn't just get in his truck and go, like he was saying he would when they spoke last night.

"Ohhhhkay," she said, pouting like I'd told her she had to eat broccoli for breakfast.

"How about waffles with syrup and strawberries? I have some fresh berries from Tony."

Lacey nodded, but her gaze kept flicking toward the hallway where Mannix's room was situated.

I turned away, not wanting to see the look of yearning on my daughter's face for the stranger for whom I too felt connected. *Way too connected.* As Reid's *younger* brother, then he was definitely several years younger than me, and it felt a little strange lusting after him the way I did.

But I had an excuse of sorts. I hadn't been with a man since my husband had died.

My daughter, however, was feeling connected to him on another level. More than anything, I hoped it was just a passing interest and not part of the fated mate link I felt toward the Alpha-born male. As my blood ran through Lacey's veins, she would naturally gravitate to Mannix as a father figure, and that seemed somehow disloyal to Evan's memory.

I hurried to the pantry and pulled out the flour, eggs and sugar.

Then a door opened from the hallway and Lacey shrieked, "Mannix! You're up! Mom's making breakfast."

I didn't turn around, my stomach suddenly so twisted up in knots it took me a minute to collect myself. I concentrated on getting out the wooden spoon and bowl, then slowly lifted my head to watch him approach.

I couldn't help but notice he moved like an Alpha, slowly, and with purpose. He exuded strength and reliability.

He'd be deadly in a fight.

"Would you like some waffles?" I managed while Lacey rushed over to Mannix and grabbed his hand, pulling him to one of the stools perched near my countertop.

I couldn't stop staring at how comfortable Lacey was with him. She'd never shown affection to any of the other men in town. She barely even hugged my dad, her own grandfather.

So, what was this?

Mannix slid onto the stool, pushing his thick dark hair back off his forehead. "Yeah, waffles sound amazing."

"Are you feeling any better?" I asked, pouring him a glass of water and giving it to him before I got back into the stirring and mixing of the waffle batter.

"Yeah, definitely." He narrowed his eyes at me as though he hadn't really seen me before. "I couldn't sense a whole lot yesterday. I was kind of out of my head, so I'm sorry if I said or did anything to offend you."

I smiled and pulled out the waffle iron. "You were totally fine."

I went about slicing strawberries and getting breakfast ready while Lacey chatted to Mannix. "Do you want to come to school with me?"

I almost laughed, but kept on cooking, interested in how he would handle a nine year old girl.

"School? Really? That's cool you guys get to go to a real school. We didn't have that where I grew up."

My ears pricked up, listening to him.

"You're lucky!" Lacey gushed.

"Oh, no, I wasn't," Mannix told her. "It meant I had to get out to work and help the pack. At your age, I was building houses and helping with the farming. I would have much preferred to be at school with my friends, learning reading and writing."

"How come you didn't have a school?" she asked.

A question I wanted to know the answer to as well.

"Well, my pack was in a bit of trouble after our Alpha died. People were unhappy, and the place was falling apart. So, I helped the new Alpha to get everything back on track. But it took a while. I was only five or six years old back then."

My heart ached, listening to Mannix explain something that would have been so tough, yet make it simple so Lacey could understand.

"Well, maybe you should come to school with me," she said. "My teacher can teach you how to read and write now."

Mannix chuckled and the deep, soothing sound rolled around the kitchen, making me shiver.

"I'd love to, Lacey, but I have to get going later today. Maybe if I come back and visit Reid again, I could take you up on your offer?"

"You're leaving?" Lacey cried. "No. You have to stay."

I served up the waffles covered in strawberries and syrup and turned to address my daughter. "Mannix doesn't live here, sweetheart. If he has to go home, we can't stop him from leaving."

"But he's meant to be here, Mom. Don't you feel it?" Lacey pleaded with me, her eyes filled with more emotion than I could fathom.

I pushed the plates toward them, feeling sick to my stomach. "You two eat. I have to use the bathroom. I won't be long."

And I ran.

When I reached the bathroom, my heart was pounding. Could Lacey really feel that sort of connection to Mannix? That didn't make any sense. Why would she?

I washed my face and brushed my teeth, needing breakfast but too twisted up inside to consider eating anything.

When I made it back to the kitchen, Lacey was packing her lunch and Mannix was slowly finishing the pile of waffles I'd put in front of him.

"You okay?" I asked Lacey, reaching for her.

She tugged out of my grip, grabbing some fruit off the table and the water bottle from the fridge. "You two are stupid," she said.

Then she left.

I stared after her, my mouth open. My daughter had never spoken to me like that. Ever.

I turned back to my house guest. "I'm so sorry, I don't know what's gotten into her."

Mannix's eyes were different this morning. They were clear, bright, alert. He was noticing things he hadn't yesterday, which likely wasn't good for me.

"I think she knows something we don't," he said quietly.

I shrugged and started doing the dishes. "Kids are funny. So, should I pack you a lunch to take with you, or what are your plans?"

Mannix stood up and glared at me. "Can't wait to get rid of me, huh?"

"Oh, no, it's not that," I rushed to say, though even to my ears my voice was too high.

Mannix crossed his arms over his chest, the muscles in his forearms bulging in front of my eyes. "Then what is it, Amelie?"

"Nothing." I shook my head. "You're the one who said you needed to leave. That Reid didn't want you here."

Pain flashed across his handsome face, and I felt instantly guilty. "I didn't mean to say it like that."

Mannix sighed. "I'll go. The only person who wants me around is your nine-year-old. Not exactly a ringing endorsement for staying."

He marched off to his room, I assumed to collect his things and go.

My heart cried out for him not to leave, and my wolf prowled angrily inside my chest. I wanted to listen to my own heart, but every self-preservation warning system rang bells in my head not to.

I had to stay away from Mannix. It was obvious he was dangerous to me.

When he emerged a few minutes later, he'd pulled on a hoodie and had his bag in his hand. "Thank you for yesterday," he managed, then placed some fifty-dollar bills on my counter.

"Oh, that's way too much," I said, rushing to grab the money and give it back to him.

"No. It's not." He walked toward my door. "Bye, Amelie."

Then he walked through my front door and shut it behind him. I was left, clutching two hundred dollars and experiencing an ache in my chest the size of Texas.

"Well, crap." What should I do?

Suddenly a cell phone went off, with a ringtone I'd never heard before.

I tucked the money into my jeans pockets and ran in search of the phone. The sound was coming from my guest room. When I went inside, the noise became louder, but I still couldn't see the phone.

Then it began to vibrate in a weird way, clattering on wood.

I dropped to my knees and looked under the bed and there it was, alight and dancing.

The ringing stopped before I got to it. I reached under the bed and grabbed it, holding it tightly in my hand. *Tony*. Probably one of his pack members calling him.

Shit. Now I had to take it to him, and just when I thought I'd gotten out of his presence.

I gripped the phone hard and walked steadily to the front door.

I could call Allara. Get her to come and pick it up from me.

But I wasn't calling Allara, and I wasn't slowing down. My body had taken on a mission of its own and I was carefully walking toward the Alpha's home.

Their place was a large, two-story house at the end of my street, and with each step I took, the band around my chest got tighter and tighter. Mannix's truck was still parked in the driveway.

Was it truly possible to escape a fated mate?

Would I be able to forget him once he left?

Would my daughter?

I was only a few feet from Allara's front door now. I could hear talking inside, growly, deep voices that indicated Reid was home too.

I took a deep breath, my chest shuddering with the effort.

Then the door burst open and Mannix trotted down the steps, his eyes flashing silver and yellow when he saw me, his wolf shifter clearly attuned to my presence.

"What do you want?" His tone was bordering on belligerent, and I blinked up at him.

"You, uh… left your phone at my place."

He glanced down at the device in my hands, then took it from me. "Thanks." He glanced at the screen. "It's my pack. They must need me."

I nodded, sliding my now-empty hands into my jeans pockets to hide my awkwardness. "Of course. You should go if they need you."

He nodded, marched to his truck, jumped in, started it and put it into gear.

This time, there was no goodbye, no wave. Nothing. He just reversed out of his parking spot and drove off, taking any hope of a future with him.

CHAPTER 7

MANNIX

I drove fast and hard and didn't look back. Those bastards didn't give a shit about me. Not my brother nor his wife, and especially not the woman who'd opened her home to me over the past day and a bit.

I'd thought there was something special about Amelie, but she'd acted like I was a thorn in her side. A pebble in her shoe. Just like Reid had.

He'd thrown a set of Alpha signature papers at me so fast I hadn't even been able to get a word out.

He'd produced them, not me. I had arrived here only wanting to find and reunite with my brother. I hadn't even considered the idea of him handing over the role officially to me, but he had. And he'd had the papers drawn up while I lay in bed at Amelie's house, nursing my migraine.

That was it, as far as he was concerned. Papers signed, and we were done. So much for a blood connection. He behaved as if I'd been the one to drop him in the forest all those years ago. But I'd been *five*. And the moment I found out he was alive, I'd come looking.

I drove and drove, until my eyes felt like they were hanging out of my head. But I didn't dare stop for long. I got gas and something to eat, and stayed on the road all night.

In the end, I made it home without proper rest. Almost twenty-four hours driving, straight. But I did it. And I managed to bring back the goddamn migraine with me.

When I arrived home, I staggered out of my truck, and people rushed to meet me.

"You're back," Tony said, putting an arm around me. "You okay?"

I nodded, my head throbbing. "Yeah. Just a migraine."

"I'll get you home." Tony started barking out orders. He was my main beta and was a great help when it came to running the pack.

I was half carried to my small house, the place I'd shared with Alfred for most of my life.

"Your room?" Tony asked, and I nodded. I couldn't sleep in the master bedroom. That had been Alfred's space.

We walked into my bedroom and Tony helped me to the bed where I sat, my vision gone in one eye. "Give me a sec." Tony closed the blinds so the room became dark and came back to stand in front of me.

"Did you find him?" he asked.

I nodded. "Yeah."

There was silence in the room, and I shifted so that I could lie down and rest my head.

Tony was still there, so I waited, but he didn't say anything.

"You still there?" I asked, because the throbbing inside my head was so loud it was very possible that he'd left, and I'd missed it.

"Yeah."

"Do you want something? Or...?"

"You can tell me to butt out if you want."

I sighed and raised an arm and rested it behind my head, attempting to get comfortable. "What do you wanna know?"

There was a beat of silence, then Tony asked, "What happened? When you met him?"

I took a deep breath, fighting the pain in my chest at the mention of my brother.

"Reid? Well, he was angry, to be frank. Couldn't believe I'd come looking for him after so long."

"Seriously?" Tony's surprise mirrored my own.

"Yeah. But he got his hands on some paperwork—or his mate did —and he signed the rights of pack Alpha over to me."

"Just like that?" Tony asked.

I nodded, then stopped because it hurt. "Yeah. Just like that."

"Wow."

I would have laughed if I'd had the strength. "Yeah, shocked me a bit, but hey... at least I know he's alive, and he's happy where he is. Now I can move on with my life."

"What was he like?" Tony asked. "I remember him a bit from when we were little, but not much."

I shrugged. "He's big, like Dad was. But quiet, like Mom. His mate is the Alpha of the Northwood pack, and although I didn't see her in action, I could tell she's pretty fierce. They'd be a formidable team to go up against."

Tony chuckled. "Lucky we're not in the mood to fight them then, huh?"

"Hmmm..." I agreed, but God, part of me wanted to go a few rounds with Reid. Pay him back for not coming home. To his family. To me.

"I better get some sleep, Tony. Come wake me in a few hours, yeah?"

"Sure, Mannix. See you then." Tony left and silence descended.

I was exhausted, on a bone-deep level. I'd spent my life fighting to undo the damage my father had done to our pack, and I needed rest. Some help, maybe.

But there was no rescue in sight. No help, other than my betas, of course. At the end of the day, in relation to my future, there was only loneliness.

Amelie

The day after Mannix left, Lacey still wasn't talking to me. She thought I was the reason Mannix had disappeared out of our lives, and she was angry.

She still wasn't telling me why.

"Hello? Amelie? You here?" my Alpha called through the open front door.

"Come in, Allara. Just in the kitchen." I was elbow-deep in apple pies, otherwise I would have answered the door.

She walked into the kitchen, her new son strapped to her chest, looking powerful and glowing with happiness. "I wanted to check on how you're doing."

"Oh, I'm fine. Just busy," I said, gesturing to the dozen pie crusts I'd already rolled out.

"I can see that." She smiled at me.

"How are you?" I asked, gesturing with a flour-covered hand to her bump. "Is he sleeping any better?"

"No." She groaned. "But Reid's a great help. He'll walk the baby through the night for me so I can get some sleep."

The mention of Reid had the smile falling off my face. "That's good."

I glanced down at my workspace and picked up the next circle of pastry. I had to keep busy. It was the only thing keeping my mind from spiraling down into the abyss.

"Want to sit down and chat for a bit?" Allara asked.

I shook my head. "I'd prefer not to stop. These tops will dry out. But we can talk if you want. Sit and I'll bake."

I gestured to the kitchen stools in front of me and Allara moved over and hopped onto a seat. "It smells great."

"That's the cinnamon in the applesauce."

I kept moving, stirring and rolling, waiting for the Alpha to say what she'd come to say.

But she just watched me silently, and I felt even more uncomfortable. "How's..." I hesitated, not even knowing what I planned to ask, but it didn't matter anyway because she interrupted me.

"Can I jump straight to point, Amelie? I have to feed the baby soon and my boobs are killing me."

I laughed. "I remember that all too well. Shoot." *Figuratively, not literally.*

I wasn't up for dodging bullets today.

"Well, I've been talking to Reid, and I think he needs to go visit his old pack."

I stopped stirring and looked up, trying to work out what Allara was about to say. She wasn't seriously sending her husband back to the pack that tried to kill him, was she? Well, I guess technically *they* hadn't. It was only Reid and Mannix's crazy father, but still, that was a hard ask of her mate.

"I don't understand."

She sighed. "Reid is angry. Like ballistic angry. I've never seen him like this. Whatever Mannix's visit stirred up in him hasn't gone away."

I bit my lip and forced my arm to move, stirring the cooking apples and watching them so they didn't turn to puree. "Well, it must have been a shock."

She nodded. "I know."

"He's technically the Alpha of his own pack," I said, musing aloud.

"I know!" Allara shook her head. "No wonder he's my fated mate."

My hand slipped off the spoon and touched the hot metal sides of the saucepan. "Shit!"

I rushed to the sink, thrusting my arm under the cold water. "That was stupid."

"You okay?" Allara called out, standing up now and rocking back and forth, probably to keep her baby asleep a little longer.

"Yeah, fine," I grumbled, the pain reducing to a throb rather than something that required a scream.

I reached back to the stove and turned off the burner. I wasn't concentrating enough to play with fire at the moment.

Then I twisted my body so I could still keep my fingers under the running water and look at Allara as well. "You really want to send Reid off to his old pack?"

Allara nodded. "Yeah, I think I have to. He needs to clear the air with his brother, and maybe put some other demons to rest. He didn't know his parents were dead either, so maybe visiting their graves would help him too. I don't know. But I know I need to do something to help him."

If what she was saying was true, then yes, she had to do something.

"Well, if that's what you think is best, then do it, Allara. Your instincts are usually pretty spot-on."

Was that why she'd come here? To bounce the idea off someone? Because if that was all she wanted...

"Would you go with him?" she asked suddenly.

My heart leapt in my chest.

I swallowed hard. "Me?"

"Yes, you. And Lacey, if you think she'd want to go."

A laugh escaped from my throat. "Lacey would go in a heartbeat. But me? Why would you want *me* to go, Allara?"

She stared at me, her eyes swirling with the silver of her wolf. "You're seriously asking me that, Amelie?"

I wrapped my hand in a cold cloth and nodded, turning off the water. "Yeah, I am."

She sighed heavily, like I was a child needing a reprimand. "Because from what Reid told me, Mannix is your fated mate. Is he not?"

Suddenly I needed to get back to my cooking. I found my first aid kit, smothered the burn in some cream, wrapped it up, and pulled on a glove to protect the skin.

When I turned back to my pies, Allara's smile was smug. "So, Reid's correct?"

I floured my rolling pin, my hand shaking beneath the stress. "Yes. He is."

She laughed, swaying back and forth. Talk about multi-tasking. "Don't make me pull rank on you."

I dropped the rolling pin back to the counter. "You wouldn't." I'd known Allara my whole life, and even though she was several years younger than me, I'd missed her when she left.

Since she'd come back, we'd become really close. But she was still my Alpha, and I'd follow her command if I had to.

"Oh, I would!" she told me. "I know I wasn't here when Evan died, but I was at your wedding. I know how much you loved him."

Tears prickled my eyes, and I lifted my arm to press the back of my hand into my nose. "I did."

"But that doesn't mean you have to turn your back on the future, hon. You're an amazing person with a heart the size of this state. You deserve to mate again. Be happy again."

I shook my head. "No. I can't. Not without Evan."

"Of course, you can." She spoke softly. "And believe me, living with the regret of letting love go is so much worse than chasing after it."

I met her gaze, and in her eyes, I could see the pain she'd suffered all those years without us, and without Reid.

I pressed both hands onto the countertop. "I don't know if he even knows we're..." I swallowed hard, forcing the words out. "Meant to be."

She smiled. "He probably doesn't, not yet. Poor guy had the devil of a migraine, and then you and Reid forced him out of the pack so fast his head is probably still spinning. Talk about a double rejection."

A double rejection? Is that how Mannix would see it? I blinked rapidly as the tears accumulated again. "Allara... I..."

"I know you're scared," she said gently. "But no amount of hiding in this pack is going to heal that wound in your heart. Love doesn't work that way."

I nodded, blinking and allowing the tears to track down my cheeks.

"Lacey deserves a chance at another family too, Amelie. You know she does. Mannix can never replace Evan, but for two people who both lost their families, you could maybe try to build a new one. Together."

I closed my eyes, not wanting to talk about the future when Mannix hadn't even indicated he was attracted to me.

Then, when I was able to, I took a deep breath and opened my eyes. She was right. The regret I felt already at letting him go was tearing me apart. Another few months... years... I'd drown with the weight of it all. And what about Lacey? If she was feeling a fraction of this hurt... "So, what do you want me to do?"

Allara grinned like the proverbial cat who ate the cream. "Well, I have a plan."

CHAPTER 8
AMELIE

Of course, Allara had a plan. She was a pack Alpha. What I hadn't figured on was packing a week's worth of clothes for Lacey and me into several suitcases, loading up Reid's truck, and then getting in.

"So, how far is this place?" I asked the Alpha's mate. Reid was definitely trembling, and not with fear.

Allara was right. He needed to do something about this rage that seemed to have him in its grip.

"About a day," he grunted out in reply.

"A day as in eight hours?" If it was, I was surprised we hadn't heard about Reid's old pack earlier. Most of the ones in the area caught up regularly for festivals and such events.

"No." He shook his head. "Twenty-four hours."

My jaw dropped open, and I glanced at Lacey in the back, already strapped in and grinning her little head off.

"Well, are we going to stop for the night?" I asked Reid, feeling like I was handling a cactus at the moment. "Or should I grab Lacey's blankets and pillows from the back?"

Reid glanced at me and all I could see was confusion and pain.

I made an executive decision. "Give me two minutes."

I ducked out of the truck cabin, grabbed food, water bottles and Lacey's sleeping stuff.

When I got back in the truck, I gave Lacey all her things, including the digital tablet and headphones I had for emergencies, and settled into my seat.

"Let's go then. We can take turns driving and sleeping."

Reid's fingers tightened on the steering wheel, his knuckles turning white.

I twisted to look at him. "You want me to drive first?"

He shook his head.

"Okay, then. Here's your water," I babbled, filling the intense silence with some inane chatter. "And I baked apple muffins and cookies to bring with us. So, they're here."

I patted the space between us, put on my seat belt and sat quietly.

Finally, Reid turned the keys and the engine roared to life.

"Let's go!" Lacey cried, her happy little voice filling the cabin. "I can't wait to see Mannix again."

I closed my eyes. *Out of the mouth of babes.*

I risked a look at Reid, and his lips had quirked into a tiny smile as he stared at me. "You okay?" he asked.

I nodded. "Yeah, let's just go."

He put his foot to the gas, and off we went.

Reid wasn't much of a talker, so I was glad I'd brought a book with me.

After about a hundred pages, I lifted my head, my stomach rumbling. "Anyone else hungry?"

"Me!" Lacey cried.

I'd packed some sandwiches, so I handed those out, happy when Reid took one and ate it quickly.

I handed him another one without waiting for him to ask. He took it and practically inhaled it also as quickly as the first. Good. Eating was a good sign.

When he finished, he glanced at me. "We'll stop soon for gas and to stretch our legs if you want."

"Yes, please."

"I need to go to the toilet too," Lacey piped up.

I laughed. "Yeah, me too, kiddo. Not long now."

We stopped for gas, used the restrooms and grabbed some junk food, then we were off again.

By nightfall, it was my turn to drive after stopping to fuel up. Lacey had fallen asleep in the back and Reid was looking tired.

"Hey, you wanna get some sleep for a while?" I asked him.

He shook his head. "I don't think I can, but thanks for the offer." He rubbed his face with his hand, clearly exhausted.

"You okay?" I asked him, not sure if he'd bite my head off, but needing to put it out there anyway.

Reid glanced in the back seat.

"It's okay," I told him. "She fell asleep an hour ago and she'll most likely sleep till we get there now."

"A deep sleeper. I like it."

I laughed. "Don't let that fool you. She was a terrible sleeper as a baby. Didn't sleep through the night until she was three. But she's making up for it now."

Reid smiled and I knew he was thinking about his baby.

"So," Reid began. "How did Allara get you to come on this trip with me?"

"You're kidding," I said. "She's Allara. How do you think she got me to come?"

Reid huffed a little. "She either cajoled you or threatened you. May have even used her Alpha rank to get what she wanted."

I gripped the steering wheel and made sure the way was clear before I overtook a truck going too slow. "You know her too well."

He chuckled. "Yeah. She usually gets what she wants."

"So, what did she do to you, then?"

He laughed properly this time, then shushed himself, looking into the back where my sleeping daughter still slumbered.

"She... well, she pulled rank. Let's just put it that way."

I didn't really want to know what she'd done to convince Reid to do what she wanted, but I was kind of glad she had.

We settled into the silence for a while, then Reid asked me, "Do you think it's true—about you and Mannix?"

I kept my eyes on the road. "I'm not sure how to answer that question."

"Just say whatever you're thinking."

I wasn't thinking a whole lot. It was my feelings that were the problem. "Well, I never thought I'd be interested in anyone again, so I'm not really sure what to think."

"Evan was a good guy." Reid spoke in that simple way that only men could do. "I liked him. He was a great pack member."

I nodded, not wanting to say anything that would encourage the tears that were currently clogging up my throat to actually fall.

"But not your fated mate, huh?"

I inhaled sharply, pain slicing into my ribs. "I... uh, thought so."

He'd been my first and only love. The father of my child.

Reid nodded. "I knew Allara was special, but it wasn't until she was gone that I really knew what it was like to live with a hole in my heart."

He coughed then, clearing his throat and pulling out a bottle of soda. "Want one?"

I reached for it. "Yeah, thanks. I don't usually have much of this stuff, but we'll need it if we're gonna drive all night."

"I might actually close my eyes for a few hours," Reid said, settling deeper into the seat. "Wake me at midnight, and I'll drive the rest of the way. Okay?"

It was only nine pm, so I didn't think three hours were enough, but I agreed, and soon enough, Reid's soft snores filled the cabin.

I smiled to myself. Despite being forced onto this excursion, it was rather nice to leave the pack. I hadn't traveled, ever. I'd never even left the state.

And as the state line came up and we were officially the furthest from home I'd ever been, a grin stretched my lips. I was closer to Mannix than I was to my pack now. I could feel it. And it wouldn't be long before I saw him again.

But what would I do when that happened? Allara and I hadn't really discussed that. She'd just told me to go with Reid and help him mend the rift with his old pack and his brother.

She'd also hinted I should open myself up to the idea of mating again.

I hadn't let a man in my bed in over five years. Getting married again? It was just so far out of my scope she may as well have suggested I go to the moon.

But we were on a mission, so I let my thoughts wander and I drove.

Around two am, just as my eyes were beginning to blur and I was considering waking Reid, he woke on his own.

"You let me sleep way too long," he complained.

I pulled over and groaned, stretching my back. "Well, you're awake now. So, swap?"

Reid raced around to the driver's side, and I crept over to fall sleep in the passenger seat.

The next time I opened my eyes, the truck slowed to a stop and the engine was then turned off.

"Are we stopping for a break?" I asked, stretching my neck from side to side, trying to work the kinks out of the tired muscles.

"We're here."

My eyes popped open properly and I blinked rapidly. The sun had risen, pink and orange shadows casting along the skyline.

"Where's the pack?" I asked, looking around.

We were parked next to a gate and all I could see was a long, winding driveway.

"Up there," Reid said, nodding his head at the gravel road. "They're pretty secretive, if I remember correctly."

"How much *do* you remember about your childhood?" I asked, undoing my seat belt and shifting so that blood flowed into all the areas of my body.

"I basically blocked everything out, but since I saw Mannix, lots of memories have been flooding back."

I didn't ask what sort of memories, but it was obvious from the twist of his lips, they weren't good ones.

"Are we here, Mom?" The sleepy question came from the back seat.

I turned to see Lacey's little head popping out above the blankets. "Yeah, we are, baby. We just have to work out how to get through these gates."

She squealed and jumped out of the truck, running over to the fence.

I went after her, panic gripping my throat.

"Mannix!" Lacey called out excitedly.

I laughed at her. "I don't think he can hear you from here."

A man came jogging down the path. "You guys lost?"

He was older, about forty, with a large scar bisecting one of his cheeks.

I pulled Lacey into me. "No. We're here to visit Mannix."

The man's eyebrows lowered. "He's not accepting any visitors."

Lacey put her hands on her hips. "He'll see me. Just tell him Lacey's here."

The man eyed my daughter like he wasn't sure if she was serious or not.

I smiled at him. "Would you mind just letting him know we're here?"

He crossed his arms over his chest, looking every bit like the beta enforcer he probably was. "Who's *we*?"

The truck's driver door opened, and Reid got out.

The enforcer's eyes widened, and his arms dropped to his sides as he took in the long-lost Alpha I'd brought with me. I guessed he was noting the family resemblance to Mannix. "Are you..." There was shock in his tone.

"This is Reid." I nodded at the hulking huge man behind me. I considered all the different ways to introduce him, since Reid had gone mute, and went with, "Mannix's older brother."

The beta raced for the gates, unlocking them with a key he pulled out of his pocket and pushing them wide. "You can drive up to the main house if you want."

I grinned at him, almost feeling sorry for him now. "Thanks..."

"Steve."

"Thanks, Steve. I'm Amelie and this is Lacey."

His lips quirked up into a half smile and we climbed back into the truck.

"You okay?" I asked Reid, who'd gone a strange red color in the face.

He nodded. "Let's get this over and done with."

CHAPTER 9

MANNIX

I was working on a new house foundation when Tony came running up to me. "Uh... Alpha... Mannix."

I wiped the sweat off my brow and stared at him. "Did you just call me Alpha? What the hell's wrong with you?"

"Uh... you have guests."

I laughed. "Guests? Why do you sound all pompous and... Oh, shit. They're here, aren't they?" *Amelie and Lacey.* I could *feel* their presence. Reid too, for some reason. I just *knew*.

I'd felt like crap up until this morning. Like, the worst hangover of my life. But I'd woken up feeling better.

Initially, I'd hoped it was just me feeling better about being home, recovering from everything I'd gone through these past two weeks. But now that I knew they were here, I wondered if they were the reason.

"Where are they?"

"Your place."

I groaned and put down my shovel. "Okay."

I jumped out of the ditch and started walking toward Alfred's house. When I realized I was alone, I turned around to gesture to Tony. "Come on. I know you want to meet him."

Tony ran after me and too soon, I was opening my front door and walking inside, muddy boots and all.

Inside, Tony pointed down the hallway. "They're in the living room."

I nodded, inhaling sharply past the sudden tightening in my chest. "Thanks."

I took one more step and Lacey came hurtling around the corner. "Mannix!"

She threw herself into my arms and I couldn't do anything but hug the kid back. "Hi, Lacey. How are you doing?"

"I missed you." She squeezed tighter.

Amelie stepped into the hallway and her gaze met mine with a clash that was heard through my entire body.

"Baby, you're gonna crush Mannix. Let him come through and talk to us, okay?"

Lacey disengaged her arms but grabbed my hand so we could walk together.

I didn't look at Tony because I could only imagine what his face would be saying.

The kids in the pack didn't really like me, and I'd never had a problem with that.

Lacey, however, didn't have that issue. And not only that, she ran through all the walls I'd erected around my heart and obliterated them like they were made of air.

I liked her. She felt... right.

"Come on," Lacey said, tugging me faster. "Reid came to see you, too."

When I stepped into the living room, Reid's presence became overly apparent. He filled the space like a bear.

"Hey," I said, lifting my chin at him.

He nodded back, not speaking at all.

I looked at Amelie, then back at Reid. "Can I help you?"

Reid made a strange, garbled groan noise and Amelie rushed forward as though to protect him. "We were kind of hoping we could stay here for a couple of days."

"Stay?" I repeated. "Here?" Since when did they want anything to do with me or my pack?

"Yeah." Amelie swallowed in a way that made her throat work. "We didn't really get to talk to you much the other day, and Allara thought—well, we thought…"

She trailed off awkwardly, and I couldn't help the wry laugh that burst out of me. "That would be right. Allara thought. Yeah, well, she would."

I stormed over to the coffee table and picked up the contract Reid had signed and waved it in his face. "You signed away your rights to this pack, so just go back to your mate and your baby, and leave me the hell alone."

My heart was pounding too hard, and my teeth were beginning to shift, the sharpness of my canines biting into my lip.

Reid stalked up to me, his eyes flashing yellow. "Outside. Now."

Oh, yeah. It was on.

I turned and strode out of my house, tugging at my shirt as I went. My brother wanted to fight me, and I couldn't wait to beat his arrogant ass.

When I hit the grass, I heard his growl.

I whipped my head around to see Reid transform into a huge, black wolf.

My own shifter leapt forward, bursting through my humanity as I transformed into my grey wolf.

I dug my paws into the ground, staring at my big brother as he bared his teeth at me.

I didn't wait, launching at him.

He mirrored my move, twisting away at the last minute so my teeth found nothing but air. I snapped my jaws at him again in warning, then flew at him.

We danced and parried. His teeth tore into my shoulder. My jaws latched onto his back.

I put all my anger and frustration into the fight, but in the end, it was Reid's strength that won out.

He pinned me flat on my back, his teeth wrapped around my neck.

I didn't whine or submit, but when I relaxed my muscles enough so that it was obvious I was no longer fighting, Reid retreated.

He shifted back to human within a few steps, then stood up, naked, blood dripping down his side and over his hip.

I got to my own feet and shifted back too, panting, pain stinging my flesh where his teeth had sunk deep.

Amelie came running out, shaking her head. "You two are idiots. Come back inside and I'll check your wounds."

Logic and reason came rushing back. "Where's Lacey?"

"She's off with Tony. He took her for a tour of your pack so she couldn't see you fighting."

I was grateful for the fact she hadn't seen me fight Reid and lose. I didn't want her thinking less of me. What did Amelie think, though?

"Come on," Amelie called, cool as a cucumber.

Reid followed her inside and I walked after him. She didn't seem ruffled, but that didn't mean anything. I'd already discovered that Amelie was a master of hiding her feelings.

She'd made herself at home, pulling out a first aid kit I'd never seen before.

"Turn around. Let me see your back." She spoke first to Reid, then grimaced when she saw the damage. "Might need a few sutures but it'll heal."

She wiped at the area and pulled out some butterfly bandages, then once she was done, walked around Reid and came toward me.

I forced myself to stand still and let her inspect me, not an easy task when my wolf liked her so much and wanted to surge forward to greet her.

When she touched me, her skin was electric against mine. "Let me just wash this. Your wolf genes will sort you out."

She touched and prodded and cleansed my burning wounds, but I barely felt any pain. Her touch made pleasure push away any other feelings.

Finally, she was done, and she stepped away. "How about you both have showers, get dressed, and I'll make us an early lunch."

I nodded, not wanting to fight with her.

I pointed toward my bathroom. "You use that one," I told Reid.

Then I walked into Alfred's room for the first time since he'd passed away. There was no way I was letting Reid use Alfred's bathroom.

The sink still had his toothbrush and as I stepped into the shower, the strange, woodsy scent that I associated with Alfred rose up around me.

Grief filled me. I stepped beneath the water and let the tears run. The pain, the despair, it all swirled around me, leaving me raw and empty. And strangely hungry.

When I emerged from the bathroom, I snuck back into my bedroom and grabbed a fresh pair of jeans and a sweatshirt.

I pulled the clothes on and headed back into the living room, finding Amelie had found what she needed from my kitchen cupboards and was cooking up bacon, eggs, and toast with butter.

"Smells incredible in here," I admitted, sitting down at the dining table. I hadn't eaten in that spot since Alfred passed away.

"Well, you had lots of food to cook up, which was good." She set a plate down in front of me and served up scrambled eggs from a saucepan. "I'll get you the toast and bacon."

She served everything right to me, just like Alfred used to, and it was like I was part of a family all over again. But this one had a woman in it.

Reid arrived then, dressed in a towel.

"Your bag is over there." Amelie pointed to the hallway, and Reid disappeared again.

I grabbed a fork and began shoveling the food into my mouth.

"You okay?" Amelie whispered as she placed some orange juice down in front of my plate.

I glanced up at her, but she wasn't looking directly at me.

"Yeah. I'm okay," I said, and she nodded before disappearing into the kitchen to get more food and plates.

Then Reid appeared and sat at the table.

Amelie set food down for him, and sat down with her own plate, buttered toast in the middle of the table.

We all ate, the fight forgotten, the air clear.

I munched on my toast and listened to the sounds of people once again filling up my childhood home.

By the time we were finished eating, Lacey had returned with Tony, and Amelie set her up with breakfast too. The woman could cook well, that was for sure.

I sat back and watched them all interacting, my heart aching in the strangest way.

I'd sworn never to have my own kids, but was I missing out on something incredible?

"Reid, uh..." Tony cleared his throat. "Can I show you the town? A lot's changed since you left."

Reid got to his feet and took his plate to the sink. "I don't remember much, to be honest." He took a deep breath, as if fortifying himself. But then he nodded. "I'd appreciate that."

He held out his hand to Lacey. "Hey, kid. How about you come with me and show me what you found on your tour."

Lacey ran for Reid. "You have to see the school! It's awesome."

Reid and Lacey followed Tony out and, soon enough, Amelie and I were alone. She leaned against the kitchen counter, looking far too beautiful.

"Thanks for lunch," I managed, dragging myself to my feet and feeling the tug of pain in my back. "And for patching me up."

"I'm just glad you didn't really hurt yourself." She bit her lip.

"Why?" I asked. When she frowned, I added, "Why would you care?"

She didn't say anything, but her eyes seemed to hold the answer.

I moved closer, standing in front of her and inhaling the sweet scent that was uniquely her. "Why do I feel like I know you? Why do I feel like..." *I want to kiss you.*

I didn't finish, but she whimpered anyway, a strange, pained sound.

I took a risk, setting the plate down on the counter behind her, then moving a little closer. I splayed my hands over her hips and stepped up.

She didn't move, and once again wasn't quite looking at me.

I reached for her chin, lifting her face gently so she couldn't help but meet my gaze.

When she finally did, there was so much uncertainty and worry in her eyes, it made me pause. "Are you okay?"

She nodded. "Kiss me, please. Before I change my mind."

I pulled back. "Why would you change your mind?" Was this about her past or mine?

She came forward, gripped my shirt and tugged me toward her, pressing her lips against mine in a desperate kiss that made every part of my body light up like the Fourth of July.

Despite the way she'd pounced, I couldn't pull away. Her taste, her heat, everything about her felt totally right.

I gathered her into my arms and moaned at the pleasure rippling over every inch of my body. My heart, my soul, my wolf... every part of me was happy.

And that's when it hit me.
Shit.
She's my fated mate.

CHAPTER 10
AMELIE

Why I'd kissed Mannix like that, only the universe really knew. But there was one thing I did know. I wanted to touch him, to *feel* the connection. I had to know if it was real, or just another trick sent to test my loyalty to Evan's memory.

I could have done the seduction part of it better, of course, but even with my awkward moves and out-of-practice kissing technique, the answer came through loud and clear. And not just for me it seemed, because after a heartbeat of blinding passion where time and space stopped and we melded together like two pieces of a lost puzzle that had finally found one another, he pulled away.

No, it was more exaggerated than that. He staggered back as though he could barely walk and yet needed to put as much distance between us as possible.

He left me standing alone, grasping at the cold air between us, while he fell backward over his couch and tumbled his way onto the floor.

Ouch... could you be any less subtle, Mannix? Was my kiss really that bad?

"Holy shit." I heard his mutter before he finally got to his feet, looking more like a drunkard walking out of a bar than a guy who'd just eaten an early lunch without any alcohol whatsoever.

"Are you okay?" I called out to him, because it seemed like the right thing to ask.

Every part of me was buzzing. My lips, my skin. Every part of me that he had touched wanted more, and every part he hadn't ached for the moment it would be their turn. I was a pile of shivering, wanting flesh. Not something I'd ever felt before and a part of me was afraid of the intensity of the reaction. Was this really how it was meant to feel?

"Uh... I... Are you..." Mannix stumbled over his words, then finally asked, "How is this possible?"

He looked as dumbfounded and as shocked as I must have that first night, I realized.

"I don't know how," I managed. "But, yes, I think you're my fated mate." The pain my heart went through saying the words was worse than I could easily describe.

Evan. I loved you. I did.

"That doesn't mean we need to act on it," I added. "But if that's what you were asking, then yes... I agree with you. It feels impossible."

Mannix stalked back over to me, his dark eyes swirling with silver, his jaw tight. "You knew about this?"

Oh, fuck.

"I didn't know... exactly. I thought it might be possible though, yes." I wrapped my arms around my body and bit my lip, not liking the angry tightness I could see in Mannix's shoulder and face.

"Then why didn't you say something?" he ground out. "Why did you let me leave?"

"Let you?" I scoffed at him. "You're not a child. You told me that you wanted to go. That you couldn't stay there with Reid, and you left."

He narrowed his dark gaze at me. "If you'd told me we were mates, I would have stayed."

I growled a little, getting annoyed now. "I didn't want us to be mates, okay? I already had a husband I loved. And a child. I didn't expect to find out that I had a fucking *mate* after everything I went through!"

Mannix's gaze roamed over my face, his hands planted firmly on his hips.

He was angry and frustrated? Well, so was I.

I wanted to run, to hide. To take my daughter far, far away, so I didn't have to deal with all the feelings coursing through me. But my wolf had other ideas. When Mannix took a step forward, my wolf rose up and took over.

She wanted her mate, and he was right in front of her. So, when Mannix tilted his head for a kiss and then froze as if fighting his own wolf, I surged up to meet him. I wrapped my arms around his neck and pulled him in tight against my body.

His lips crashed down on mine and a groan sounded loudly in the room. His or mine, I didn't know, and I didn't care. I just needed to get closer, to feel loved, to feel alive again.

Mannix grabbed my ass and hauled me against him, but it just wasn't close enough. I wanted the heat of his skin against mine.

I tore at his shirt, and he pulled up my t-shirt equally roughly.

When he stumbled back, he grabbed my hand and pulled me with him. I didn't ask where we were going, I just let him lead me to his bedroom, where we undressed each other between frantic kisses. I got down to my underwear and Mannix was fully naked before I even knew what was happening. My wolf knew, though. She was humming with excitement and a sense of rightness.

I couldn't help but stop and stare, just for a moment. He was so beautiful. Muscled and smooth, with just the smallest sprinkling of hair across his pecs.

He reached around me for my bra fastening and I stopped him, uncertainty filling me for the first time. I was seven years older than him, and I'd had a baby a long time ago. My body didn't look like the girls I was sure he was used to bedding.

"Um…"

"What's wrong?" He pressed a kiss to my neck, a low growl reverberating against my skin.

"It's just… you know. I've had Lacey, and my body's not twenty-one anymore."

He lifted his head and stared at me. "Amelie, all I can see is you. And you are beautiful. You're my *mate*."

Hot tears sprang to my eyes because that was exactly how I felt about him.

I reached behind me and unclipped my bra, letting it slither to the floor.

Mannix's grin lit up his whole face as he slid his fingers into my panties and dragged them down my legs to the floor, kneeling before me as I stepped out of the circle of fabric.

But Mannix didn't get back up. He simply grabbed my ass with his hands and pulled me in closer.

"Oh… ah…" I wasn't sure about him doing that. Not yet.

But he didn't listen to my fears. Instead, he kissed me. On my belly, on my hips, then moved to lick between my thighs.

I gasped at the pleasure and heat that shot through me as his tongue found its mark.

He pulled back and grinned up at me. "Lie on the bed for me, Amelie."

I turned and rushed over to the bed, lying down on the mattress before I could let my fears run away with me.

He crawled over, prowling up between my legs and pushing open my thighs. He didn't even hesitate. He set his mouth directly onto my clit, making me buck and squeal, straight into his waiting tongue.

I gasped out as he held me steady, working his lips and tongue and teeth over my flesh. The sensations were so intense and incredible. It was like being whipped around in a storm of pleasure. I had no control, simply holding on for the ride.

He kissed me and worked my flesh until my stomach tightened and I was crying out to him to stop. To keep going. To do... something. I couldn't even think straight anymore.

Then he moved upward, leaving me aching and wanting.

He kissed my belly and then my breasts, stopping to suckle on each of my nipples. I threaded my fingers through his hair, holding him to me. I wanted to love on him as he was doing for me, but I had the feeling he wasn't going to let me. Not this time, anyway.

He lifted his head and slid his body up along mine. I moaned at the feeling and opened my legs further as he settled between my thighs. His cock was hard and thick against my belly and my core ached to be filled by his beautiful flesh.

I tugged him down to kiss him, meeting his flaming lips with my own. He kissed me deep and hard, his tongue mingling with mine and letting me taste him in the most fundamental way—with his mouth coated with my own essence as well as his own unique flavor.

Unable to think, I could only feel as he moved against me. I clung to his shoulders, digging my nails into his muscled flesh. The urge for him to be inside me was overwhelming, so I lifted my legs, wrapping them around his hips and moving my pelvis until his cock nudged my entrance.

That's when he lifted his head and stared down at me, his eyes almost pure silver now. His wolf was close to the surface, as was mine. "You sure?" His voice was hoarse with the effort of holding back.

I didn't want him curbing his desire anymore. "God, yes." I found myself wanting to beg. "Please."

He shifted slightly, nudging me softly. But I groaned and pushed against him, needing so much more.

He moaned, then thrust hard.

I cried out as his cock forged a path inside of me. Opening me up and setting me alight. Claiming a part of me I'd long forgotten existed.

He froze, allowing me time to adjust, then as I sank my teeth into his shoulder, he finally began to move.

Slowly at first, just rocking against me. He withdrew almost all the way, until I was digging my nails into his arms to pull him back. Then he drove into me hard, leaving me breathless.

He fucked me long and hard and deep, sending rivulets of pleasure through my body and tears to my eyes.

As he moved faster and his own gasps and groans grew more intense, my belly tightened and heat coursed down my legs.

"I'm going to..." I managed to gasp out just as Mannix roared above me. He thrust deep and came inside me.

His orgasm triggered mine and I screamed out as wave after wave of pleasure buffeted my system. My belly trembled as my pussy rippled around his cock, dragging every last ounce of sensation out of both of us.

We lay there for long moments, his weight on top of me and the sounds of our heavy breathing filling the air.

When he lifted himself up and slowly rolled off me, withdrawing from my body in a way that made me feel instantly empty, I rolled onto my side and faced him. He put his head on the pillow and stared at me.

Neither of us spoke, and I could see the worry mounting in his mind.

"It's okay." I reached out to cup his jaw.

He rolled onto his back away from me and stared up at the ceiling. "Amelie, that was the single most amazing moment of my life, but I am *not* okay."

Despite being afraid that I was about to be rejected, I crawled across the space between us and nestled into him, putting my head on his chest and feeling the thump of his heart against my cheek.

He didn't push me away. In fact, he put his arm around me and pulled me in tighter.

"Do you want to talk about it?"

He shook his head. "Not really."

"All right." I closed my eyes and tried to ignore the gnawing pain seeping into the bliss surrounding us. I wanted to be happy, even if it was just in this one moment. Because, to me, what we'd just shared had been more perfect than I ever dreamed possible.

MANNIX

How was I going to tell Amelie that I couldn't mate with her? That my family line was cursed and there was no way I'd risk my father's crazy genes being perpetuated in the future.

Part of me wondered as I lay there on my back with my mate wrapped in my arms, that maybe it wouldn't come to be. That just maybe, I could escape it. Reid had, after all. He'd found a mate, and an Alpha, at that. He'd had a child, and he didn't seem to be afraid that child would turn out like our dad.

But Reid wasn't the Alpha of my pack, and he looked nothing like our father. He may have had Dad's size, but in appearance he was all Mom. So maybe his bloodline wasn't tainted like mine.

Everyone said I was the spitting image of my father. And I wasn't risking my child's health or my mate's. If I was destined to go insane like Dad, my betas had orders to put me down. Fast. Before I killed anyone.

I would *not* turn out like my father.

But I had no idea how to even broach all of that with Amelie. Instead, I released a loud sigh.

"I'm going to have a quick shower," I told her, kissing the top of her head because I couldn't stop the compulsion.

"Now?" Amelie grumbled, sounding half asleep.

I rolled out of bed and tried not to notice how gorgeous she was. How soft her hair looked as it fell across her face. "Yeah. I won't be long. You just rest."

She nodded and curled back into the pillow, pulling the blanket up over her naked shoulder.

I backed away, then rushed into the bathroom and shut the door. My heart was pounding like an enemy pack was on my heels, and sweat broke out on my forehead.

What had just happened with Amelie... that wasn't meant to happen at all.

I flicked on the shower and let the water warm up. Steam filled the room. "Oh, God." What was I going to do?

A growl rolled through my chest as inside my mind, my human and shifter personalities fought against one another. My wolf wanted me to go back into my bedroom and make love to Amelie again, but I couldn't. I just couldn't. She'd never understand why I wouldn't give her children or fulfil the role she'd want me to play.

I stepped beneath the hot water, washing away the scent of fear and anger. Fucking *Fate*! How dare she tempt me like this? Put my mate right in my path when I wasn't able to marry her and make her truly happy. Not the way she should be.

Picking up the soap, I washed myself from head to toe, then dried myself off and snuck back into the room. Amelie was fast asleep, so I grabbed a t-shirt and jeans and headed out into the living room. The whole house smelled like her, and my cock responded accordingly.

I groaned. "Fuck."

The front door opened, and Lacey rushed in, laughing loudly.

Reid raced in behind her, his relief palpable when he saw that I was dressed and alone. "Sorry… she got away from me."

"All good." I nodded to Reid. "Thanks for giving me the time to… err… chat with Amelie."

"You two okay?" His gaze was curious.

I nodded. "Yeah. She said she was tired and needed a nap."

The edges of Reid's lips tilted up as though he knew exactly why she'd fallen asleep, but when he turned to Lacey he said, "Your poor mom drove half the night getting here. She was probably exhausted."

Lacey came up next to me and grabbed my hand. "Can we go get something to eat, Mannix? I saw a restaurant that had hamburgers."

I laughed and grinned down at the little minx. "They make amazing burgers. You wanna go?"

She nodded and gripped my hand tightly. "Yes, please."

Reid sat on the couch, yawning loudly. "I might catch a few zzzs, too. You okay with her?"

"Yeah, of course," I answered, before I even thought about it. Lacey was a great kid, and I had no problem spending time with her.

She tugged on my hand and pulled me outside. We chatted on the way to the café, and soon we were sitting in a booth holding identical burgers and sharing a big basket of fries.

"Mannix?" she asked.

I glanced up. I knew that tone. I was about to be asked a probing question. "Yes, Miss Lacey?"

"Why don't you have kids?"

I laughed to hide my awkwardness and put my burger down so I could take a sip of my soda. "Well, for one, I'm only twenty-five, and that's young to have kids."

Especially for an Alpha male.

She tilted her head. "Do you want them?"

"Do I want kids?" I repeated, stalling a bit as my heart began to thump a little too hard. "Well, I'm not sure."

I *was* sure. I didn't want them. Not my own, anyway.

She took a big bite of her burger, looking thoughtful, and then grinned. "You like my mom, don't you?"

I grabbed a handful of fries and squirted ketchup on them. "Why are you asking?"

She shrugged. "I don't know, it's just... I think Mom likes you and I don't want her to get hurt."

I swallowed hard, the intensity of the little girl's gaze rivaling that of an Alpha wolf. "I don't want to hurt your mom either, sweetheart." Especially after everything she'd been through already.

Between us, I'd lost my parents, my brother and my stand-in dad, and Amelie had lost her husband—who she clearly adored—the father of her child.

We were the walking wounded.

"Promise?" she asked. Lacey seemed too old for her years, but I knew from experience that losing a parent could do that to a kid.

I nodded. "I'll try my absolute best not to hurt her, I promise." I wasn't sure if that was possible but I'd try to let Amelie down as gently as I could.

"Okay." Lacey shrugged and focused wholeheartedly on her meal.

When we finished, we went for a walk and chatted like friends who'd known each other for years. I wasn't sure how Amelie had raised her to be so wise and fun, but she'd done a good job.

After an hour or so, we meandered back to the house. Amelie was sitting on the doorstep, staring at us with big, soulful eyes.

She stood up as we got closer and reached an arm out to her daughter. "Hey, Lacey."

"Mommy!" she cried and ran into her mother's arms. "We had burgers!"

"That's very nice," Amelie said, though her voice was thick, and I could tell she was struggling to speak. "Could you go inside and play on your iPad for a little while? I need to chat with Mannix."

"Really?" Lacey asked, her mouth practically dropping open. "Yes!" Then she ran into the house.

Amelie turned to me, thrusting her hands into her jeans pockets. "She doesn't get a lot of screen time."

I nodded. "You've got a great kid there."

"Yeah, I think so too." She seemed to change her mind about her posture and crossed her arms over her chest instead. "I think we need to talk."

I didn't want to because I could already feel where this was going. "Probably not a good idea."

She glared at me. "And why is that?"

I looked up at the sky and clasped my hands over the back of my neck. "Ugh..."

How could I even start to explain my situation?

"Mannix. Look at me."

I dropped my arms and did as she asked.

"What are you so afraid of?"

It was time to tell her the truth. I took a deep breath and let it rush out of me. "I can't give you what you want, Amelie."

"Really?" She lifted a mocking single eyebrow. "And what is it you think I want?"

"A mate," I said simply. "More children."

A strange sort of hurt flashed across her face.

"You do, don't you?" I asked. "Want all those things."

She didn't answer but I knew she did. From the pinch in her lips to the yearning in her eyes.

"Well, I can't give that to you," I told her. "I mean... I want to... but you have to understand. I can't."

"What do you mean, you *can't*?" Her voice was a whisper. "Are you married already?"

"Me?" I practically scoffed. "No! Of course not."

"Have you..." She swallowed hard. "Can you *not* have children?"

I glanced away so she couldn't see the regret in my eyes. So many times I'd almost gone to get a vasectomy so I wouldn't be able to have a child, but I'd never had the courage to go through with it.

I swallowed hard and managed to meet her gaze with mine. "I don't know. I've never tried."

"Then what are you talking about?" She covered her face with her hands for a moment before dropping them and sighing.

"Let me get this straight," she went on. "I finally face up to the fact that the father of my child wasn't my mate. That I had another decreed by Fate in this world and I've finally found him, and you… you… what? Just don't want me?"

"Of course, I want you!" I ground out. "But can't you see I'm bad news? You don't want to be the Alpha's mate in a pack like this. Our bloodline is cursed. *My* blood. It's cursed."

"Bullshit!" Amelie hissed. "Reid has a mate *and* a son! You're just afraid."

"Of course, I'm afraid!" I practically screamed. "My father murdered my mother and tried to murder Reid and me! Don't you understand? He *killed* her. And would have killed me if it wasn't for Alfred. And Reid, if it wasn't for Allara's pack. Don't you understand that? He was crazy. And I'm just like him."

"You're not like that!" She poked me in the chest, hard, but her eyes were full of tears. "So, what's that got to do with you and me?" Her lips were trembling. "You can't possibly think that will happen to you."

I looked away, fighting my own heartache and finding it impossible to meet her eyes. "It's not safe, Amelie," I said, more quietly now. "You should go. And take your daughter with you. Lacey shouldn't be here, either."

The front door suddenly flew open, and Lacey came running inside. "You're a liar! And a coward." The accusation in her gaze was almost my undoing.

My heart broke and I staggered a little as my knees almost went out from under me.

The pain I saw in those eyes, I knew too well. "Lacey, I—"

"No!" She thrust out her hand at me as though she could stop me from walking forward. "Don't say anything. If you don't want to be my new daddy, you don't have to be."

The tears were welling up in my eyes now. "Sweetheart, I..." I would have loved to be her stepfather. I hadn't even thought about that as a possibility.

She was right. I *was* a coward.

"Lacey, he's not..." Amelie tried to help, but her daughter made a wounded, angry noise, and ran out of the room. Out of the house and down the front steps.

I watched her flee into the town and beyond. I'd hurt her. An innocent child.

"I better go after her." Amelie walked past me with the tears in her eyes beginning to fall down her cheeks.

"I'll come with you."

"No!" she said, with the same unbending tone Lacey had used. "You've made your position clear. We'll be back soon to say goodbye."

Then she, too, walked away from me.

CHAPTER 12
AMELIE

I stomped off down the road, so angry and hurt I didn't know if I should let myself cry or fight through the impulse. My heart ached and my throat burned with the most terrible sensation. After so many years of grieving my husband's death, I would have thought I had no tears left. Or that I'd at least be used to the pain of loss. But no... this was a whole new fresh level of agony.

I swallowed hard and blinked rapidly, deciding that I wouldn't cry. Not today. Maybe tomorrow. After all, my mate—my true, fated mate—had just rejected me. I was entitled to a few tears, surely, but I'd handled worse, hadn't I? I could handle this, too.

I'd get through it. My daughter, however, might not. I'd never heard her speak to anyone like that before, nor had I ever heard her so upset.

She'd been too young to even remember her father. It was me that kept his memory alive for her by telling her how great he'd been, how much he'd loved her. But Lacey didn't actually remember having her daddy, and now the man she'd obviously secretly been hoping wanted the job had rejected her as well.

It was "broken hearts for all" day, it seemed.

My gaze scanned the village, searching for her among the houses, old and new. The roads weren't in the best shape, but the people grew small gardens around their homes, and I could smell baking and fresh bread in the air.

They were rebuilding, that was obvious.

"Oh! Lacey!" I called out to my daughter when I spotted her sitting on a big rock, her arms wrapped around her knees. "Honey!"

"No! Go away!" she yelled back at me before taking off, running between two of the houses and toward the forest.

I froze in place, tears welling in my eyes and falling onto my cheeks. "Oh, baby, I'm so sorry."

I wanted to go after her, but my legs wouldn't move, and the weight of my daughter's pain made it impossible to stop the tears now. How was I going to explain this to her when I didn't even understand it myself?

Mannix had gone through a lot, that was obvious. But he was letting fear stand in the way of his future, and a few days ago I would have been right there with him...head in the sand and feet firmly planted in denial.

By the time I realized Lacey really was heading into the forest and not stopping at the edge, she was gone. Damn. I shouldn't have let her go like that. She'd disappeared right into the trees, and I couldn't see her at all. The good news was she couldn't shift yet, so she couldn't have gone far. She'd probably just find a log to sit on, and mope for a while.

I took a deep breath and exhaled slowly. I had to get a handle on these emotions. I was a mother first and foremost, which meant my disappointment could be processed another day. Today, I'd pack up and head home with or without Reid. Lacey and I were out of here.

I turned and walked back to the house where only an hour ago I was making love to Mannix.

I shook the thought out of my head and walked straight through the open door. Reid was there, waiting patiently on the couch, and the moment he saw me, he jumped to his feet. "You okay?"

I shook my head. "No. It's time to go home."

"Now?" he asked. "We only got here this morning."

I knew what he was saying. We were both exhausted and couldn't make another drive like the one we'd just done.

"I know, but I got what I came here for. Answers. What about you?"

Reid glanced across the room, and I assume he was looking at his brother, but I couldn't do it. My heart was banging way too loudly in my chest, and all I wanted to do was get away from here. I ignored Mannix altogether.

"Uh, yeah. I suppose I did," Reid admitted. "But I don't think we should drive straight home."

I shrugged. "No problem. I'm sure there's a motel not far from here. We'll sleep there tonight and take our time driving home."

I lifted my chin even higher as I felt the heat of Mannix's gaze from across the kitchen. "Give me an hour to pack up and make sure I've got everything, Reid. Then we can leave."

Not that I'd unpacked, but between the three of us, I was sure our shit had spread from the car to the house and elsewhere.

"Where's Lacey?" Mannix called out, forcing me to turn my head to look at him. He was standing in the kitchen, leaning against the counter.

"In the forest. She ran off after you rejected us, and I decided to give her some space." Or that was my excuse anyway. Shock and heartbreak had been the real reasons I hadn't bolted after her. "As soon as I'm packed, I'll go find her."

Mannix's eyes narrowed at my words, but he didn't speak.

Reid coughed awkwardly, clearing his throat. "I have a few things I still need to talk to Mannix about."

"You do that." I walked over to the couch and picked up Lacey's iPad. "I'll get the truck ready."

I bent my head so I didn't need to look at either of them anymore, and set about collecting the things we'd already scattered. Sweaters, toys, water bottles.

The men wandered off and I heard them speaking in hushed tones out front. I tuned them out and focused on getting ready. Within fifteen minutes, I was pretty much done.

I walked outside with the final bits and pieces I'd gathered in my arms and looked at Mannix, trying to keep my expression blank. "Thank you for having us." I dragged my gaze away from the pain I saw in his eyes and met Reid's gaze instead. "You ready to get home to your wife and baby?"

I couldn't seem to resist the final dig at Mannix.

His main argument seemed to be that because their father was an asshole, he was destined to be one too. Ergo, no wife or baby, or even a mate.

Well, Reid had done it all and I couldn't see Allara rolling over if Reid suddenly became an asshole. Quite the opposite.

Mannix shuffled his feet. "Amelie, we have to talk."

"No," I snapped. "Unless, of course, you have something new and more positive to say?" I looked at him then and raised my eyebrows since my arms were full.

"Uh…" He stopped, then shrugged.

"Didn't think so. Okay, then. I'm gonna drop this stuff off, then go find my daughter." I twirled on the balls of my feet and headed toward the car. He didn't *want* to change his mind, that was obvious. If I was ten years younger or Lacey wasn't in the mix, maybe I'd stick around just to see if I *could* change his mind.

But I wasn't young and dumb anymore, and I had a daughter to protect and care for. I'd already endured the death of my husband

and was raising Lacey by myself. If Mannix wasn't man enough—hell, if he wasn't *Alpha* enough to stand up and want me on my own merit—then he could go get fucked.

I repacked the truck with the few things in my arms, then marched back to where Reid and Mannix were still talking.

I looked at Reid, ignoring Mannix. "I'll go fetch Lacey and meet you at the truck."

Reid nodded and I turned to go, but that was when a couple of Mannix's betas ran up to us, looking worried. "Mannix! Bear shifters. In the woods."

I staggered sideways, the weight of those words hitting me hard. Not bears, damnit. No. Not when Lacey was out there alone.

My husband had been killed in a battle with bears. They were huge and vicious, and took no prisoners.

"Seriously?" Mannix was already ripping off his shirt. "But we haven't seen them for months."

"I know. But they're back and they're obviously looking for trouble."

Mannix growled. "Fuck. Okay, round up the troops, and head to the forest line. Now!"

He went to race off, and I had to stop him. I launched forward and grabbed his arm. "Who are these bear shifters?"

"Enemies." His eyes had already shifted, and his teeth began to change right before my eyes. "I need to go, Amelie. Defend my pack."

I would have rolled my eyes if things weren't so deadly serious. He was being all Alpha and perfect now, was he?

We had to get out of here. *Now.* I wasn't losing another member of my family to some bears. Oh, holy hell. Lacey!

"Okay. But which direction are they coming from? Which area of the forest?" I could barely breathe, the reality smacking me in the face. "Not the little section to the west, is it? Like, behind those houses over there?"

He nodded. "Yeah. Why?"

No! Not my baby. No. Please.

I threw the truck keys through the front door, toward the couch, not caring where they landed.

I began to strip off my own clothes. I had to get to my daughter, and I was faster in shifter form. "That's where Lacey ran off to."

A growl erupted from Mannix, and his human morphed instantly into his wolf.

"Oh, shit." Reid said, before a feral growl ripped through him as well. His shift was only slightly slower than Mannix's.

I let my own wolf take over, my maternal panic making my human self useless.

Mannix was already gone. His black wolf disappeared like lightning down the street, on his way to save his pack. And hopefully, to help protect my daughter.

CHAPTER 13

MANNIX

I raced through town, the sounds of growls in the distance making me push myself harder. We'd fought these bastards a few times over the years. They were a natural enemy, and the bears had always wanted our land.

We beat them back every time, though we lost men whenever we faced them. I didn't want to lose anyone else, but that wasn't the fact that had my heart pounding in my chest today. It was Lacey. She was out there by herself, and I couldn't endure the thought of something happening to her.

She was Amelie's daughter. And that made her special.

Please, Lacey. Walk back out of the forest. Now. Please.

I hit the boundary of our town where some of my betas were yelling and already corralling women and children into their homes.

We'd practiced this a hundred times. They knew what to do.

I threw back my head and howled, calling any remaining pack members to the fight.

Reid was suddenly beside me. My brother. At my shoulder, ready to support me. I would deal with that thought later but for now, we ran together into the dense treeline. My wolves were everywhere, and I yipped at Reid. He seemed to know what I meant, and moved to the left, running along the boundary, looking for Lacey.

I could hear the cries and growls of the bears, which were quickly approaching.

I darted through several trees and into a nearby clearing, looking around for the little girl who'd been so disappointed that I didn't want to be her daddy.

God. What had I done?

I'm coming, sweetheart.

I ran along the tree line, bolting in and out, looking for a little girl with dark hair. I wanted to shift back to human, just so I could yell out her name, let her hear me call. But I didn't dare turn back. Not with bears on the loose.

When I got to the top of a small rise, I looked down the other side, and that's when I heard her cry.

"Help me! Please! Helllpppp!"

I squinted into the distance and caught sight of two huge Kodiak bears loping through the trees. Just ahead of them was Lacey, running for her life. Those bears were toying with her. Having some fun before they stepped it up and took her.

I didn't hesitate. I raced down the hill toward her, howling and growling as I went.

As I got closer, I could see the terror in the little girl's eyes. I pushed harder when she tripped, falling down into the mud and scrabbling along beneath the trees on her hands and knees. Like her mother, Lacey was clearly a fighter. She would not give up.

When I reached her, I leapt, sailing over the top of her head and landing on the other side of her body.

I planted my feet firmly and growled as loudly and viciously as I could.

I didn't look behind me, but I heard Lacey panting, scratching at the earth with her fingers.

Run, Lacey. Run!

I lowered my head and growled as the brown bears came loping along on all fours. They stopped the moment they saw me and stood up on their hind legs.

I glared up at their forms. They were now close to eight feet tall.

Unable to hear Lacey anymore, I hoped to God she was gone, running back toward the village and safety. Relief sailed through me even as the bears dropped down onto their front paws once more and readied to attack.

If this was my time, then it was my time. But I'd go out of this world knowing my girls were safe. Amelie and Lacey. My girls. My family. And I'd managed to get to know my brother once more, even if it was only for a few days. That was something.

Amelie

My wolf caught wind of Lacey's scent and I raced through the forest, searching for my baby.

I reached the top of a small cliff. Now Mannix's scent also wafted on the breeze.

And suddenly, there she was, running through the forest toward me, her dark hair blowing behind her like a flag. Lacey!

I ran for her, down the hill and beyond. When I was within ten feet of her, I shifted back, collecting my daughter into my arms and holding her tightly against me.

"Thank God, you're all right." I cupped her face and pulled up her chin so I could look at her properly. "I was so worried about you, baby."

"Mannix saved me," she sobbed, tears tracking down her cheeks. "Two bears were chasing me, but he covered me so I could get away."

Two bears? A howl and a lot of growling sounded in the distance, and I pulled my daughter in to me. "We need to get out of here. Quickly."

We turned just as Reid's wolf ran up, shifting as he went. "You found her. She's okay?"

I nodded, pulling Lacey into my side. "She is. But she said two bears were chasing her and Mannix is now fighting them off." I bit my lip to stop the sob that rose. To lose two mates to bear shifter attacks... I wasn't sure I'd survive a second time. "You need to help him, Reid. Please. He..." I trailed off, unable to finish, and Reid nodded.

He pointed through the trees. "That way?"

Lacey sobbed. "Yes. Please go help him."

Reid leapt through the air, shifting on the fly.

Lacey surged in the same direction, obviously wanting to go after him, and I understood her compulsion. I wanted to go after Reid too and help battle the bears. For Mannix, and to assuage my own demons. For Evan.

But I had to get my daughter to safety, and if two Alpha wolves couldn't take these assholes down, then my assistance would be moot. If Mannix and Reid lost, then we were doomed

Blood dripped into my eyes from a gash on my head, but I ducked a massive paw swing and managed to get away once more.

I could have taken down one bear myself, but with both working in tandem, it was getting harder by the minute to stay alive.

I ducked again, ran around the larger one, and snapped at his heels. His claws came swinging around and I darted back.

Shit! How the hell was I ever going to take these guys down? I couldn't run because I couldn't risk endangering anyone else in town. But I needed help.

The answer came in the form of a huge black wolf, sailing over a log and running at full tilt toward me. It was Reid.

My brother has my back.

Warmth filled me even as Reid flew at the other Kodiak, tearing into its neck and chest.

The bear bellowed and the one I'd been fighting turned to help its comrade. I took a chance and launched my own renewed attack, tearing at the bear's hind legs and tasting blood running between my teeth.

Reid and I pounded into the bears, over and over, tearing at them, biting them, and taking over the fight. With two of us, there was hope in my chest instead of despair. We could do this. Together.

The beast fighting Reid suddenly turned tail and fled, running back into the forest in classic retreat style. The Kodiak I was fighting glanced after its friend and when I released my jaw's hold on his right back leg, took off as well.

I limped over to Reid and stood side by side with my brother, watching the bears run away. He didn't look too injured. He had some blood on his fur and a chunk of ear missing, but overall, he was the poster boy for surviving a battle.

I, however, was a different story. I was beginning to see spots.

Turning, I began to limp back toward town. I couldn't hear any snarling, vicious bears any longer. No howls of pain or anger. There was only silence in the forest.

Did that mean all the bears were gone? I had to find out. I needed to check on my pack and find out if Lacey had gotten back to Amelie okay.

I trudged forward, ignoring the pain in my head and legs. It wasn't far to the top of the hill. I could make it. Surely, I could.

Halfway up, I knew I couldn't. My wolf wouldn't continue any longer. I had to shift back and get some help for these injuries. I let go of my wolf and groaned as the levels of pain ratcheted up twenty-fold in my human form. "Oh, fucking hell."

Reid was beside me, instantly shifting back to human also. "Come on, brother." He spoke as calmly as one would on any given day. "Let's get you home."

He put his arm around my waist, and I managed to throw my arm over his shoulder. Together, somehow, we made it back to town.

"Thanks for the help there," I finally told him. He was taking a lot of my weight, but still allowing me the respect of being able to walk on my own two feet. "I'm not sure I would have made it without the support."

Reid, the big lug, shrugged. "Happy to help."

I wasn't sure what else to say, so I just nodded and kept going. I had to find out if Lacey got back to her mom safely. "Do you think she's okay?"

Reid glanced at me. "Lacey?"

"Yeah."

"Yep. She's fine. She was the one who told me to come find you."

Relief sailed through me, and a piece of the puzzle fell into place. That's how Reid had found me. Made sense. "Oh. Good."

"You shouldn't have gone after the bears alone." His voice was a little darker and crankier now.

I laughed; I couldn't help it. He sounded like me when I was annoyed. "Yeah, well... I can see the insanity in it now. But when I saw those bears chasing that kid..." A growl rolled through me. "I wanted to kill them on sight."

"Yeah, I must admit," Reid said, "I know that feeling. My son isn't even walking yet, and I'm terrified something might happen to him."

We'd reached the edge of the trees. My pack and town lay only a few yards away, and yet my legs were screaming at me not to continue. Black swirled at the edges of my vision.

"I think I have to sit down."

"No, you don't." Reid grabbed a tighter hold and forced me to continue walking down the street and into town. "Your people need to see you're alive and well."

I nodded and clenched my jaw tightly, hearing my teeth click together. He was right. I knew it.

"Just push through," he said. "We're not far away now."

Somehow, we made it. Reid managed to get me home, and my betas all came rushing to see me.

"Mannix! Fuck, man. You okay?"

I nodded as Reid got me to the front door of my house. "I'm fine. How's the pack? Did we lose anyone?"

One of my betas, Tommy, shook his head. "Nah. We did good. A few injuries but overall fine."

"Great," I told him, beginning to sink lower and heavier against Reid. "I'm gonna get patched up, and I'll see you guys later. Come get me if anything else happens. Okay?"

The ran off cheering, elated with the win.

I was happy for them, but I'd be even happier when I could finally sit down. Or better still, lie down.

"Oh my God. Are you okay?" Amelie came running to the open front door and threw one of her arms around me, stabilizing me on the other side of Reid.

"Yeah. I'm fine." I really couldn't see that well now. "Just need a few stitches, I think."

My legs were wet with blood, and I wasn't sure where it was all coming from. My back hurt and I was pretty sure I'd taken a bear claw to the belly at one point, but I wasn't risking looking down. Not yet.

"Let's get him inside, Reid." Her voice was quiet. Concerned.

I mock scowled at her. "I'm still here, you know."

"Not for long," she said. "These injuries are gonna make you pass out soon. I don't know how you're still standing."

I didn't either. "I needed to find out if Lacey was okay."

Then Lacey herself bolted into the room, her eyes wide with fright. "Oh, no," she whispered.

"I'll be fine, sweetheart. Don't you worry. Your mom's gonna fix me up."

My vision had narrowed. I squinted in her direction but couldn't really see the young girl much at all.

"Lacey, go find the first aid kit in the truck, okay?" Amelie's voice was sharp. I could hear the underlying fear. *Hmm. I must be pretty bad then, I guess.*

The youngster nodded, then bolted out of the house.

The moment she was gone, the world went dark.

AMELIE

After Mannix passed out, Reid threw him over his shoulder and carried him as fast as he could into the main bedroom. The room still smelled like sex, and the sheets were rumpled but there was no time for embarrassment now.

That wound in Mannix's stomach looked pretty bad. And the one in his back wasn't much better. He'd already lost so much blood.

"Here you go, Mom." Lacey panted as she ran back into the house with my first aid kit in her hands.

"Thanks, sweetheart. Could you get me some clean water and put the kettle on?"

She nodded and raced out of the room.

Reid hovered over me. "Do you think he's going to be okay?"

"Yeah, of course," I muttered, barely able to breathe through the worry and tightness in my chest. *I hope so.* "We haven't finished our argument yet. He can't die before I have my final say."

Tears leaked out my eyes, belying my attempt at humor, and I brushed them away.

Reid put a hand on my back. "Just hold on a bit longer, Amelie, you're doing great."

I nodded because my throat had closed up and I couldn't speak now. He couldn't die on me. He wasn't allowed to. That wasn't how this was meant to work.

If he didn't want me or my daughter, then fine. But he was *not* dying. He was *not*.

I pushed all feelings aside and focused on my role, assessing his injuries and blood loss. The outlook wasn't great.

"I'm going to need to do some stitches. Do you think you could stay and help me in case he wakes up?"

Reid walked around the bed to stand by Mannix's head. "What do you want me to do if he does wake up?"

I lifted my gaze from the mess of oozing claw marks and managed to smile. "Knock him out again."

Reid didn't smile back, just nodded grimly.

When Lacey brought me back some bottles of water, I thanked her and sent her away. It was a tough couple of hours of sewing flesh together and wrapping wounds, but I did it. He'd come home to me alive. It was the least I could do for the man who was my fated mate, whether he wanted me in his future or not.

When I was done, I fetched some clean blankets and draped them over his nakedness.

"What do we do now?" Reid asked.

"We wait." I wiped my forearm over my sweaty brow.

"You want to go take a shower?" Reid suggested.

I stared down at my hands, where dried and fresh blood both gathered on my skin. "Yeah, thanks."

I was exhausted. There was no other word for it. Emotionally, mentally, physically. There was no way we were driving away from this town tonight.

Lacey was sitting on the ground by the front door and, as I walked over to her, I noticed people outside. "What's going on, sweetheart?"

"The betas are here to check on Mannix." She calmly gestured to the front door.

I walked closer and glanced outside. There were people everywhere.

The men who'd been sitting on the porch obviously chatting with Lacey on her level, jumped to their feet. "Is he okay?"

"Is Mannix alive?"

"Will he be okay?"

All the queries came at once, and I noticed, not for the first time, that not many of them referred to him as Alpha. Whether that was by choice or by Mannix's decree, I wasn't sure, but it was unusual for a pack to have so much respect for their leader but not call him by his proper rank.

"He's alive," I announced, and a general cheer went up around the group. Women in the back hugged each other and two of the men surged closer.

"Can we come in?" They put their hands to the door.

"He's sleeping," I said, raising my hands to show them the mess I was in. "He lost a lot of blood, but I've patched him up the best I can. I'm going to have a shower, then I'll check on him again."

"Please." The guy at the front said. "Just us two. We need to see him."

I glanced at the two betas and tears filled my eyes once more. I knew that feeling. That deep-seated gut ache that made you desperate to set eyes on the person you loved, just to reassure yourself that he or she was still alive.

To watch them breathe. To see their chest rise and fall.

I'd never gotten that with my husband. He'd been dead by the time they brought him back to me. So, to have this moment where Mannix was alive, and I'd helped to heal him... it put parts of me back together that I'd never thought was possible.

He really was my second chance. At everything.

I'd almost lost him and my daughter in the same day.

"He saved my life," Lacey announced to the two men as they opened the door, then shut it after them. "The bears would have eaten me for sure."

I backed away from them, struggling to breathe again. "Sweetheart, you walk them through what happened, okay? I need to grab some clean clothes, then wash."

I pushed past the group and ran for the truck where I grabbed out my suitcase once more. Then, feeling the burning gazes of the pack on me, I ran for the safety of the shower.

There, within the tiled walls, I bawled my eyes out. For everything we'd all lost. For the pain we'd been through. For the fear that still crippled every choice we made.

Mannix. Me and Lacey. Even Reid, who'd been left to fend for himself so young. All of us had suffered in the past.

The hot water washed away all the blood on my skin, and I scrubbed my nails until they were red from the vigorous cleansing. I could still feel it on me, everywhere. So, I stayed under the water, washing every part of me until the water ran cold.

Finally, it was time to get out and face them.

I snuck out, changed into clean clothes, then found the house to be quiet. The pack had gone. There wasn't anyone waiting on the doorstep any longer.

I went looking for Lacey and Reid, only to find them both sitting by Mannix's bedside. "Has he woken up at all?" I whispered into the quiet room.

Lacey jumped up and ran over to me, straight into my open arms.

"It's okay, baby," I whispered, holding her close. "It's okay."

"He's going to wake up, right?" she asked as she pulled away.

I nodded, though my certainty at that point was wavering. "Of course, he will. He has Alpha blood. They heal the best, you know. Isn't that right, Reid?"

I turned toward the Alpha in the room, who nodded silently.

"Is it okay if I go play outside?" Lacey asked.

"You can," I said, "but stay close to the house, okay?"

She nodded. 'Oh, don't worry. I'm never going into those woods ever again."

I smiled at her as she left, then collapsed into the chair by Mannix's nightstand that she'd vacated. "Any news?"

Reid ran a hand through his rumpled hair. "Just got the report from Mannix's betas. The bears all retreated, and quickly. It sounds like Mannix has trained his pack well. They fight together, as a team. They do drills every week to keep them all fit and strong."

I tilted my head and stared at my Alpha's mate. "You sound proud of him." Reid had been fighting the connection to his brother since the day Mannix had turned up on our pack's doorstep.

Surely, he could see that it wasn't Mannix's fault Reid had been abandoned as a child?

"I am," Reid said, though the words were stilted. "I just—"

"What?" I prompted. "Can't get past the fact that he didn't come for you earlier?"

Reid glanced away and I knew that had something to do with it.

I sighed. "Well, that would have been a bit difficult, given he thought you were dead. I think you're blaming the wrong person, Reid."

"Yeah. I am," he said finally. "I should blame myself."

I groaned with frustration. "What are you talking about? You two were kids. *Kids*! Your father is the only guilty party in this, Reid. Not you. Not Mannix. You managed to survive and went on to be our Alpha's mate. Mannix survived and looks like he's doing a pretty good job of getting this pack back on its feet."

Reid nodded and I could see the shimmer of unshed tears in his eyes.

"Why should you blame yourself, Reid? You're not making any sense."

"I should have tried to find Mannix," he admitted. "He was just a little kid. It wasn't his fault our father was a fucking psychopath."

I rolled my eyes. "Try telling him that! He thinks he'll turn out just like him."

"What?" Reid asked, turning toward me. "What do you mean?"

I lifted my legs up onto the edge of the seat and wrapped my arms around my knees. "Mannix told me he's cursed. That he can't take a mate or have kids in case he wakes up one day and tries to kill us all."

It sounded crazy to me, but Reid nodded like he understood.

"Oh, not you too?"

Reid grinned at me. "We're all afraid of having a mate and children. Especially when you're an Alpha."

My jaw dropped. "Seriously? I would have thought it would be the opposite. That you guys would be driven to procreate. To continue the line."

He chuckled. "Yeah. You'd think so, huh? But instead, you worry about adding to your responsibilities. Mannix already feels responsible for his pack. Every man, woman and child. He worries about disappointing them. About failing them when they need him most. Adding a mate and children to that... well, not every man is built for it."

I lay my chin on my knees. "So, I should give up then?"

Reid laughed louder this time. "Hell, no, you don't give up. You two are fated mates. You'll never be happy without one another. Trust me, I know."

I smiled at that one and closed my eyes, leaning back in the chair and willing sleep to descend on me also. Reid had been separated from Allara for six years after her father had deliberately broken them up. Neither of them had done very well alone.

"Thanks, Reid."

I stayed in that chair, drifting in and out of sleep for the rest of the day and all night. I didn't leave Mannix's side because something told me that if I left, he wouldn't be there when I came back.

CHAPTER 15

MANNIX

When I woke up, early morning rays of light were filling my bedroom. I hurt, everywhere, but I was alive. And that was a start.

I blinked rapidly, my eyes adjusting to the half-light. And there she was, sitting in a chair, curled up and asleep. My mate.

I struggled to sit up and pain sliced through my belly, making me hiss. Fuck, that hurt.

Amelie sat bolt upright, blinking her big eyes like an owl. "You're awake!"

I groaned. "Barely."

She jumped to her feet, dashing over to the nightstand. "Have some water. Do you want something to eat?"

I managed to drag myself up to a seated position and rested against the backboard. "I'm fine, but how's everyone else? Where's Lacey? Is she okay?"

Amelie handed me a glass of water, smiling tentatively. "Everyone else is great. Lacey's fine, thanks to you." She slumped into the chair before me. "Thank you for saving her life. I would never have gotten there in time."

I took a sip of water. "Yeah, well, I didn't have a choice there. My wolf just took over."

She nodded slowly. "The Alpha in you, I suppose. Needing to protect a child."

It had been so much more than that. As I'd taken on those bears, all I could think of was that Lacey had to get to safety. She was too important to lose, and she was well worth losing my life over.

"Ah… yeah," I managed.

I didn't know when we'd get the time we needed to sort everything out, but I didn't want Amelie leaving. "Will you stay for a while longer? I know you were determined to go home—"

"I'll stay," she jumped in to say. "At least until you're back on your feet." She glanced toward the door. "Lacey likes it here. She's made friends with some of the other kids, and Reid is finally letting himself talk to some of your pack members."

"What do you mean, he's letting himself?" That was a strange way to phrase it.

"Well, I think he was partly afraid to get to know any of your pack. You know—in case they blamed him for leaving or staying away, or something."

I nodded slowly. "Yeah, I hadn't really thought about how he'd feel with all this."

This was meant to be his pack. His people. Instead, he'd ended up making another pack his home.

"He's getting better," Amelie noted. "I'm sure Allara is absolutely busting to get up here, so she'll come visit too. I'm positive of that."

I smiled. "Fine by me."

I moved each part of my body slowly, checking for injuries. My feet, my legs, my arms, then my torso. There were a lot of aches and deep wounds, but my head was clear. I was healing well.

"Did you patch me up?" I asked. We didn't really have doctors in town anymore. Some of the women could manage basic first aid, but that was it.

She nodded. "Yes. You needed some stitches, so I hope that was okay?"

I chuckled and sighed. "Yeah, it's amazing. Thank you. You always seem to end up taking care of me, don't you? First the migraine, now this."

She reached out and ran her fingers through my hair. "Yeah, well... you need someone to take care of you. You can't look after everyone else all the time and not receive any nurturing in return."

I turned my head, leaning into her caress. It felt so damn good. "Mmm..."

I hadn't had anyone look after me like this for as long as I could remember. While Albert had been a great mentor and surrogate father, his response to any type of injury or migraine scenario was more of a "suck it up" type of mentality.

"I'll go make some breakfast." She stood and began backing toward the door.

"Could you send Lacey in?" I called out. "When she's awake. I need to apologize to her."

Amelie stared at me, her look unreadable. "Ah... sure. Okay."

Then she disappeared.

I lay there in bed, regretting everything I'd said to Amelie yesterday after we'd made love. Here was a woman who'd already gone through so much, and I practically tossed her out of my bed and told her I could never mate with her.

Who wouldn't want to marry a woman as beautiful and selfless as she was?

I was an idiot. A fool.

And I was going to make it up to her.

I tested each of my joints, moving my arms and legs to get the blood pumping again. Amelie had done a good job of sewing me up, because I could feel myself healing with each minute that passed.

There was a soft knock on the open door and then Lacey walked in, hesitating just inside the doorway.

"Come on in, sweetheart. Have a seat."

She slid onto the chair, her big eyes focused on me. "Are you okay?"

"Yeah, of course I am."

"You saved me," she whispered. "Thank you."

I reached out and grabbed her hand, then tugged her over so she'd sit on the bed next to me. "It was my fault you ran off. I upset your mom and I upset you. And I am so, so sorry about that."

She nodded her head and began to cry. I pulled her into my arms and hugged her, letting her cry out whatever tension she'd accumulated over the past few days.

"I'm so sorry, Lacey." I hugged her tightly. "I'm so sorry that I ever made you feel like I didn't want to be your stepfather. That was never my intention."

She pulled back and stared up at me. "Does that mean you want to be my daddy?"

I took her hand in mine and squeezed her fingers. "I'm not sure," I said, and her smile fell.

I grabbed her hand again when she tried to pull away. "I don't mean it like that. I mean..." I sighed. How to communicate this with a nine-year-old? "My father wasn't very nice. And I'm worried that I won't be a good one to you."

She tilted her head and stared up at me. "But you're nice. You're nice to me, to your pack. Was your dad like that? Did kids like him? Did his pack like him the way your betas like you?"

The question was so simple but turned my world on its head. "Well…"

Everyone hated my dad. Everyone was afraid of him.

"Do you know that when Mom was stitching you up, your whole pack was waiting to hear the news? Your betas sat on the porch and talked to me, and there were women and children everywhere."

"Uh…"

"Doesn't that mean they like you? Respect you? Like our pack with Reid and Allara. Everyone respects them."

My throat tightened. "Well, to answer your question, no, I don't think the pack liked my dad very much at all."

I was too little when he died to remember exactly how everyone reacted to him, but I did remember the fear. And the ripple effect of what he'd done to his people still went on to this day.

"Then you're not like him." She jumped off the bed to stand next to me. "So, you can be my daddy, and Mom and I can stay here."

Then she pointed her little finger at me and squinted her eyes to make it look like she was glaring. "But you need to say sorry to Mom. You were mean to her. And she doesn't like it when people lie."

"Lie?" I repeated. "I didn't lie."

That was one of the things I stood for. Complete and utter transparency. It was the only thing I had some days.

She walked to the door, then turned back to face me, a happy little smile on her face. "You promised me you wouldn't hurt Mom and you did. And second, you said you can't protect me and you did."

Then she skipped out the door, taking my heart with her.

I sat there for too long, mulling over everything she'd said, the expression *out of the mouths of babes* swirling around in my mind.

When the door opened again, it was Amelie, with a plate of bacon and toast. "Are you hungry?"

I nodded. "Yeah, thanks."

I needed to eat and gather my thoughts, and then it would be time to jump with two feet into the life I was meant to lead.

CHAPTER 16
AMELIE

I couldn't eat. My stomach was in knots. But I drank my coffee and watched Mannix eat his breakfast.

"I'll go clean up," I said, standing and walking toward the door.

"I'll take a quick shower, then meet you out there," he said, swinging his body around and planting his feet on the floor. He winced as though the movement had hurt him, which it probably had.

"You should rest," I told him.

Mannix stood up and smiled at me like it was any other day. "I'm healing quickly but feel dirty. A shower will do me good. I promise I'll make it a short one."

I nodded, not sure he was right to jump straight into showering, but it was his call. His body. "Okay."

"Then, can we talk?" He stared at me with a hope, an innocence, that I'd never seen in his eyes before. My heart leapt. What did that mean?

I couldn't say anything except, "Yeah, sure." But my pulse was racing like a runaway train all of a sudden.

Then I opened the door and slipped out, a squeal of nervous excitement building in my chest. What did he want to talk about? Obviously, it would be about what had happened between us, but what did he want to say now?

Had he changed his mind? And how did I feel about that?

I knew I couldn't leave him, not now, maybe not ever. Being away from Mannix would almost kill me. The connection I could feel building between us was growing by the day. Every minute I was with him, the pull toward him got bigger and stronger.

There was no going back to how we were before, but could we move forward in a way that would make us both happy?

Could he love Lacey and me? Could we build a life together amidst the ashes of our pasts?

I didn't have to wait long to find out. By the time I'd cleaned up the kitchen, checked on Lacey and texted Allara to give her a quick update on what was going on, Mannix was out of the shower and standing before me, his hair still wet.

He looked pale but better than earlier. "Do you want to sit down?" I gestured to the furniture.

He nodded, looking far too gorgeous for a man who was on death's door only yesterday. "Sure."

I hurried over to the couches and sat on one while he sat on the other.

"Where's Lacey?" he asked suddenly, glancing toward one of the windows at the front of the house. "Is she still playing outside?"

I nodded, a little surprised by the question. It had been a long time since someone other than I cared where Lacey was or what she was doing. "Yeah, she really likes it here."

"I'm glad."

The silence stretched between us until I finally asked, "What did you want to talk about, Mannix?"

"About us." His words were simple, but his tone held loads of meaning.

"Us?" I repeated, sitting straighter and taller in my chair. "Yesterday you were pretty certain there was never going to be an us."

"Yesterday I was an idiot."

I laughed out loud at that one, especially as he delivered the statement with such a deadpan expression. "Ah, you were a bit," I said. "But you also saved Lacey, and that wasn't an idiot move. Not at all."

It was a hero move, no question.

He nodded slowly. "That's what's got my mind all twisted up."

"Which part?"

He ran his hands up and down his thighs, groaning softly. "I convinced myself that I was never going to have a mate or children because the risk wasn't worth taking. The risk of..." He swallowed hard, then continued, "Turning out like my father. But then you two showed up and you both want me in your life."

I shrugged, trying for nonchalance. But inside, my heart began to race. "Yeah." *And we still do.*

"I'd never thought about the fact that I could be a stepdad or an adoptive dad, or something like that."

My heart squeezed tight, but I pushed through the feeling. "You can. Lacey wants you to be whatever you want to be to her. It doesn't mean you have to marry me or anything." Now it was my turn to swallow against the lump closing up my throat. "We can work out some sort of compromise, I'm sure."

Mannix pinned me with the intensity of his stare, then slowly shook his head. "I don't want to compromise."

My hopes fell. "You don't?" Maybe I was wrong. Maybe he didn't want us. Maybe... "Oh, what are you doing?"

He stood up suddenly and walked over to me. "I want everything," he said, and then went down onto one knee, kneeling before me.

I grabbed for his hands to pull him up. "You'll hurt yourself. Your wounds. Your stitches."

He squeezed my fingers and smiled, resolutely remaining in that position. "Amelie, will you stay here with me? Live with me? Marry me? Accept me with all my faults and failings, and... everything?"

My jaw dropped and I stared at him. "But you said..."

"I know what I said." He sighed and shook his head. "I was afraid. I'm *still* afraid."

"Then what changed your mind?" I had to know.

"Lacey," he said simply. "When I found out the bears had come to attack again yesterday, I instantly got ready to fight for my pack. Die for my pack, if necessary. Something my father would never have done. So, there's that. We're at least different on that level."

I nodded, not speaking, not wanting to interrupt him when it seemed he was on the path to enlightenment.

"But when I learned Lacey was missing and in the path of danger, I turned my back on my pack and ran for her. In that moment, she was more important than me or the pack I thought were my family. She was everything. And I know that's because she's your daughter. She's a piece of you, my mate. And if you'll have me, I want her to be *my* daughter too. Not to take her own father's place, of course, but..."

He shrugged and for a second his eyes glistened, as if he was trying to hold back unshed tears. "I want us to be a family, Amelie."

I fell to my knees in front of him, humbled by his words and by his obvious emotion. "You don't have to do this, Mannix."

He cupped my face and held me still. "I don't know if I will ever be able to have kids of my own, sweetheart. That is still my biggest fear. Would you still accept me if Lacey is the only child you ever have?"

Tears gathered and slipped down my cheeks. I hadn't thought anything he could say would have topped his first declaration, but he just beat it.

"Of course, I will." I wiped at the tears. "I'd love to have your baby, but if Lacey is enough for you..."

"She is," he said. "She really is."

"Then let's do it." I smiled despite the tears still coursing down my face. "Lacey and I will move here, and if you're still sure, we'll get married."

Mannix slowly got to his feet, tugging me up with him. "My town is still rebuilding," he said, as though warning me of something terrible. "It's been my life's work to repair the damage my father caused."

"I want to help you," I said, feeling inspired in a way I'd never felt before. "With schooling and anything else you need."

Mannix's lips tilted up. "Being an Alpha's mate in this pack won't be easy."

I laughed, happiness filling me. "I've never chosen the easy way, Mannix. I want you. I want this town. I want my fated mate."

He whooped and picked me up into his arms, squeezing me as tightly as he could, given his injuries. When he pulled back to stare into my eyes, he smiled and then he kissed me, hard.

I wrapped my arms around his neck and kissed him back, relief flooding me, enhancing the happiness in my heart. He wanted me! He wanted Lacey! We could work everything else out, I was sure.

He walked us into his bedroom, then sat down on the bed.

I pulled back and stared at him. "Are you sure you're well enough for this?"

He began tugging at my clothes, so I undressed as quickly as I could then helped him remove his clothing too. "I'm definitely well enough for this," he said. His enormous erection showed me exactly how well and how ready he was.

As I climbed up onto the mattress beside him, he chuckled. "Though, you might need to be on top for this one, sweetheart."

I speared him with a look that hopefully conveyed to him exactly how much he meant to me. "With pleasure, my mate. But first…"

I wrapped my hand around his shaft, enjoying the hiss of his breath as he exhaled sharply. "Lie back and let me pleasure you," I whispered, my eyes feasting on his beautiful body.

His eyes darkened, and he complied, lying back on the mattress and watching me avidly as I began to pump his flesh. I fisted his shaft, up and down, fast and then slow, still learning what he liked. And then I couldn't resist, bending my head to take the tip of his cock into my mouth.

His taste exploded over my tongue, and I swiped at him greedily, wanting everything he could give me, and then some. I went deeper, taking all of him into my mouth and throat, loving the sound of his groans above me. Those sounds of pleasure incited my own arousal, and my pussy dampened as if in readiness for the coupling to come.

When his groans became more feral, less controlled, and his hips began to move and buck beneath me, I pulled back. "Amelie," he huffed, his voice raspy with need. "I have to be inside you, my beautiful mate."

Every cell in my body was screaming out for more. I lifted my head and met his heated gaze. "Exactly what I was thinking, my love."

I sat up and threw a leg over his hips, positioning my pussy channel entrance just above the head of his cock. "I'll try and be gentle," I promised, and he chuckled, albeit a touch hoarsely.

"Not too gentle, please," he said. "I'm a shifter, don't forget. We heal fast." And then his words turned to another groan as I slowly lowered myself onto his hot, hard cock.

The sensation of him inside me, filling me up, was so intense I let out a tiny cry. His hands tightened around my hips, fingers clenching as he steadied me. Then I began to move, riding my mate, slowly at first and then faster, as our moans mingled together, and the delicious scent of sex rose around us.

"Jesus, Amelie, this is... God, this is *perfect*," he managed, and I gasped as the pleasure began to rise higher and higher.

"It is," I cried out. "It's like my soul is becoming whole again. Oh, Mannix, I..." I couldn't finish the sentence, could only ride the orgasmic wave as it crested and crashed over me. As I shuddered violently, my inner muscles clenching around him, Mannix released a muffled yell and came inside me in a rush of heat. And then I was off again, shuddering in yet another climax right on the tail end of the last. The intensity of it all, rushing on and on through my body, shook me to my very core.

I collapsed against his chest, forgetting about his stitches for a moment, but it didn't matter. His arms came around me and held tightly, not letting me move until our heaving breaths began to slow. He shifted his head then, smiling at me before he took my mouth in the most beautiful and intimate kiss I'd ever experienced.

When he released my mouth, tears gathered and fell. I couldn't help it. There was so much emotion racing through me that there was no other way to express it.

He reached out with his tongue and gathered up my tears, one by one. "I hope they're happy tears, beautiful," he whispered, and I smiled tremulously.

"They are. I am very happy, and I can't wait to start our new life here with you, and make a future for us, and for Lacey. It will be beautiful, I know. Because we *are* mates, and this is meant to be."

Mannix's eyes shone as he held me, and I knew that everything would be all right now that we were both on the path that Fate had decreed for us.

The path to love and happiness.

EPILOGUE

AMELIE

Five years later

It was Mannix's thirtieth birthday, and I'd raced around all day making preparations. Our new town hall was built, and I'd filled the place with balloons and streamers. The walls were lined with tables and chairs, and the pack had been cooking for two days.

After years of hard work, rebuilding and care, the pack village was looking amazing.

Allara and Reid and about twenty others from my old pack were coming for the party, and they'd be here soon.

"Hey, Mom. I finished the cake. Where do you want it?"

I turned around and grinned at my fourteen-year-old daughter. She wanted to be a pastry chef and was ridiculously skilled at making desserts. She'd created a three-tiered chocolate explosion of a cake for her stepfather.

"Wow, sweetheart, it looks amazing. Can you put it on the big table up the front near the stage?"

My strong daughter, who had recently begun shifting, carried the cake up to the front of the room. I stared after her, not for the first time feeling overwhelmed by the pure weight of how much I loved her.

Mannix and Lacey were closer than ever, and these days she called him Daddy. She had done it from the moment we told her we were going to get married.

"Hey, beautiful, how are you feeling?" Mannix asked, walking up behind me. "You didn't seem too well this morning."

I twisted around and grinned up at him. "There's a reason for that."

He frowned. "You mean exhaustion? I know you've been killing yourself to get this party done. And the school. And everything else you do."

I laughed and threw my arms around his neck. "I love our pack and everything we've achieved."

And we had achieved a lot. I'd talked to other packs in the area and managed to get help, and we had developed relationships with allies who had helped us rebuild. Our pack had grown with marriages and babies—except in our family of three.

Mannix had been quite happy not to have a child of our own for the first few years, but about two years ago, I'd gotten pregnant accidentally and then miscarried. The disappointment we'd both felt had made us both realize that perhaps our family wasn't quite complete yet.

Two years on, and I'd never been pregnant again. Until now.

"Then what's the matter, beautiful?" he asked.

I glanced over to where Lacey was still fussing with the cake. "I was thinking I'd tell you tonight, at the party, but maybe now is better."

He frowned and I knew he was beginning to worry. "What is it?"

I pressed my lips together, holding my breath. I'd been waiting over a month to tell him, but after the last miscarriage, I wanted to be sure.

"I'm pregnant."

His eyes went super-wide, then his mouth dropped open. "But..."

"But what?" I said, going up on my toes to kiss his lips. "It's not like we've been preventing it."

Mannix still made love to me each night. We couldn't get enough of one another, and I thanked the universe every day for bringing my fated mate to me.

"But... I thought..."

"Yeah, I thought so too." At thirty-seven, I'd assumed that my biological clock had ticked its last tock. "But we were wrong. I'm definitely pregnant."

"How far along?"

I tried not to smirk when I answered. "Almost ten weeks."

"What? You waited all this time to tell me?"

I shrugged. "I wanted to tell you on your birthday." And I was afraid to go through another loss with him. The last one had devastated my big, strong Alpha.

"Uh... oh..." He seemed to be totally out of words.

"Are you happy?" I asked.

He nodded and swallowed hard, his throat working with emotion.

"Happy birthday," I managed before he tugged me in for the sweetest kiss ever.

"Ew... gross. You two need to get a room."

I pulled back and laughed, tugging Lacey into our group hug and told her the good news.

"Really?" she exclaimed, her eyes going big and wide. "Oh, Mom, that's so awesome!"

Mannix pulled her into his side. "You know nothing will change with us. We still love you more than anything, and you are still my heir. The next Alpha for our pack."

Pride swelled in my heart. The day Mannix had taken Lacey as his official heir had made me fall in love with him, all over again.

She rolled her eyes, but I could see the relieved smile on her lips. "I'm happy to share the role, Dad."

We pulled her into our group hug once more, then Lacey left to go meet up with some friends.

"I can't believe we're going to have a baby," Mannix said, pressing a flat palm to my belly.

Happiness burst out of me as I cuddled into my mate. "Do you want to tell the pack tonight or do you think we should wait?"

"Oh, I'm definitely announcing it tonight." He beamed from ear to ear. "And speaking of which, I better go check on the alcohol delivery. It's due any minute."

He stopped to kiss me once more, then walked off. There was an added little spring in his step, and I was so happy I'd been the one to provide that for him with my news.

I watched him go and couldn't stop myself from cupping my own belly with my hands. It had been worth hiding my morning sickness and waiting for the right moment to tell him. The perfect birthday present for Mannix.

Now I just had to wait thirty more weeks, and our baby would be here. Fate willing.

THE END

www.ingramcontent.com/pod-product-compliance
Lightning Source LLC
Chambersburg PA
CBHW071019180726
48291CB00004B/1531